6555
Sec Cor 485040
381538

THE DUCHESS'S

DRAGONFLY

THE
DUCHESS'S
DRAGONFLY

Niall Duthie

PHOENIX HOUSE
London

First published 1993
© Niall Duthie 1993
Phoenix House, Orion House, 5 Upper St Martin's Lane
London WC2H 9EA

Niall Duthie has asserted his right under the Copyright
Designs and Patents Act 1988 to be identified
as the author of this work

A CIP catalogue record for this book is available
from the British Library

ISBN 1–897–58030–4

Typeset at The Spartan Press Ltd,
Lymington, Hants
Printed in Great Britain by
Butler & Tanner Ltd
Frome and London

CONTENTS

Foreword 1

THE ENGRAVINGS
1 The Duchess's Craft 9
2 The Duchess's Guest 14
3 The Duchess's Picture Gallery 18
4 The Menagerie 21
5 A Duchess's Supper 24
6 The Howdah 26
7 The Housekeeper 29
8 A Goddaughter 32
9 Twice Said 35
10 The Farthingale 39
11 The Seamstress 41
12 And the Red 44
13 *Más el Levante* 47
14 The Dune Pool 50
15 *La Siesta* 53
16 Selena 58
17 The Duchess's Dressing Table 60
18 The Monkey's Revenge 65
19 A Monkey's Ant 70

20 *La Banderillera* 71

21 Saint George 75

22 *Cuadros de un Zíngaro* 77

23 The Bath 80

24 The Stocking 83

25 The Marauder 85

26 The Dune Cart 88

27 The Horse Stables 91

28 The Umbrella 93

29 You've Servants 97

30 *Ce n'est pas Cuit* 104

31 Rise 107

32 On a Lapdog's Death 110

33 The Pyramid 113

34 The Senior Lady 116

35 *Mono Reconociendo a una Duquesa Echada* 119

36 Up 123

37 The Hook 124

38 *¡Que Oficio!* 127

39 I Measure 129

40 The Monkey's Mother 135

41 The Troop 141

42 The Duchess's Dragonfly 162

for Angela

FOREWORD

THE FORTY-TWO ENGRAVINGS HERE RECALLED (WITH AN
effort that racks *my* belief) were lost in a fire itself spectacular
enough to incite a few commentators, those with the lubricous
fatuity of the arsonist, into finding analogy on the ardent
personality of their owner. Not my point at all.

Still, the fire took and there is little harm (despite
Sr Maldonado, M. Lyotard and Mr Birdwhistell) in briefly
picturing a vast, not-quite-finished, neo-classical palace burning
against an Iberian nightsky: see seeping grey smoke, billowing
black plumes, the ecstatic leap and lick of huge orange and red
flames escaping from the central windows, pick out the overshadowed row of tiny figures and buckets and then imagine, inside, to
the roar of combustion and the underlying squeak and splutter of
wood-juices, the run of quick-tongued fire along fifty feet of loft
floorboard towards a sixteenth-century trunk with pale, almost
bleached-looking, leopards rampant round the locks. Picking
over the ashes a week later, someone stumbling on the vaulting
comes across a cold green and black bubbled lump, the size of an
ostrich egg and the hardness of a fossil – all that remains of once
separate, skilfully-marked sheets of copper.

In consequence, it is worth insisting: I am not recalling
impressions on pieces of paper but the metal engraving plates

themselves. That, in turn, these are not only the mirror images of prints – have the artist's signature erutangis – but that the scores and incisions on the copper are, as it were, raw. Those intended shadows, that soft drape, that wind-tugged cloak are, in the first place, filagrees of bright scratches. That glossy pit? An open mouth. That gouge and small, gleaming moat? An eye.

Put side by side in front of you 1) a plump sheet of paper about an inch wider and longer than a folio and 2) the corresponding plate. On the paper imagine some blackish marks. Look closely at where the weave has taken ink, at where the fibre has merely been touched. You see the difference? By contrast, the metal is like a brilliant mould for some relief map, but the relief is on a plane no deeper than the surface skin on pond water nor thicker than the veined wing of my favourite insect.

Of course I cannot swear that the runnels never clogged with ink, that no proofs were ever taken. But there is no press here, I have come across no blackened rags and I know that my Duchess formally asked for the ownership of the plates (when she already had possession of them) and that the artist was as sufficiently obsequious as to agree to such an exclusive transaction. 'Your Grace, Your Correspondence' – a note in *her* blobby hand, a short while before having the etchings trunked and removed.

Some 245 by 350 mm, the plates were all the same size and remain so in my mind, though, naturally, they are neither quite as stiff nor as sharp as the originals. Memory-stubbed? Not in any waiving way. It may always be, I suppose, that I have docked a tail or forgotten one of the pack but I have certainly not suppressed persons or toyed with the compositions, deliberately tilted an arm or shifted a foot. No, I merely mean that I notice differences amongst them, in them, that I cannot attribute entirely to the artist. Some are remarkably statuesque. Others are impossibly imbued with colour – mostly vein-blue and rage-red. Others, by constrast, seem seen through rain, with an uncertain pulsing of light. A few, despite my provisos about paper, appear to have curled and yellowed. And a very few seem to have beyond the frame a different world, belong to a different series. Think of a new window let into an old wall. Think of my narrowed eyes.

The artist himself, leg jig-jig-jigging, fretted a great deal over the order of the etchings. I have already mentioned a view of the series as an epistolary rejoinder, but I have found it more useful to consider it as an account that became an accounting. He was to shuffle the plates, a sighing, clanking, ragged-edged business, like a grim, old patience player, before finally numbering and titling them *en suite* a very short while before he left. The principal moves he made are conveniently indicated but all the hesitations and replacements are not. In any case the order was never revolutionised; his sense of irony was close to his sense of indignation, frequently puzzled, finally stubborn. He did, once, give a twist to a figure, once, very slightly change the composition in another engraving. These I have indicated where appropriate, giving the final version inside the brackets, mentioning the earlier version outside.

And the relation of the commentator to this process? Well, the artist is, I speak generally, not normally the subject nor the nature of art and attempts to make him so are, though only sometimes, as amusing as organ-grinding. Except, that is, in the case of self-portrait. The self-portrait here is very sly and nimble and has had recourse to me, my level, my perspective. I – and this must, if not unique, be extraordinarily rare amongst commentators – am in each etching and was never, ever changed. Let me be clear. This is

3

fez not face (*faz*), fate not faith. I love pistachios, dusting the salt off them, prising apart their lippy hardness to get at the green-tinged nut, but hate cracking either shell, leaving the nut imprisoned in a kind of bed or boat.

If this double traffic is hard to understand, then let me explain again. The artist made use of my figure and, in turn, I now find myself, the invisible, palpating bits, commenting on his use. Have you ever seen a starfish suck a mussel's shell apart and ingest the bivalve? It has five strong limbs and an extrudable stomach.

My new role, clambering about outside the plates, may be, like that unfair stomach, an imposition. So be it. At least I am aware that my remembering is an act of hubris which carries its own punishment. I would also point out that I was indeed a hairy little devil whose form was commissioned – in some engravings – to make mischief in sacrosanct places. But in the end she gave the etchings their chance. And I take it now – because I loathe fire, those bubbles in the copper, the colours in the combusted gases. Without me there is not even a semblance of the images he scratched and it is that – the fear that I may forget what was released by flames – that makes me try to refix them now.

Well, well, that is enough *punto seco*, enough dry-point. Like most artists' models I am not another artist, am almost wholly and happily ignorant of the history and technique of art. For me the affair was, outside acid and sugar, a six-week interlude. I have had a great many other weeks and many other interests. For example? I have already mentioned pistachios and starfish. But, in general, let us say natural history. And in particular? Pond life. And specifically? My marvels. My dragonflies.

The dragonfly belongs to the order of insects called *neuropter-ous*; that is, it has four membranous wings with reticulate neuration. Reticulate is to be divided into a network and neuration refers to the distribution of nervures, the tubes that form an insect's wing. Yes, but that removes the gleam and does not even help those who cannot distinguish a dragonfly from a damselfly. This is quite easily ascertained. The former is larger, the latter hold their wings up over the back when at rest while dragonflies spread theirs out sideways.

But there is a more important difference for me. The local name for damselflies is *caballitos del diablo*. Ignore the *diablo*-devil; I am almost sure that *caballitos* refer to seahorses (*caballitos del mar*) and their slow, stately progress. For, of course, though I can enjoy watching a dragonfly wait, long truncheon tail cocking, the disproportionate eyes – yellow-green pulses – alert, my chief delight is in watching them fly.

Molto andante. These voracious hunters at shimmer and whirr! That triple mounting of the air that always – ankle, knee and thigh – makes me rise. A dragonfly is *ten times* faster than a damselfly, a dart compared to a slow-spun coin.

Now, it is undoubtedly true that I have not the means nor the science nor the imagination to decipher their airy hieroglyphs. Also that some dry-point readers will say that there is nothing to decipher, that the creature moves as a consequence of beating its wings, is borne by the wind, corrects its trajectory towards whichever of its simple appetites has been stimulated and that no further design is needed. It flies for food. It mates in chains.

I disagree. Poor philosophy perhaps but good sense. The imagination is gold-veined. Those wings beat doubly. The air is a rich cloth. I enjoy the quick stitches most.

Though a dragonfly, bumping against a windowpane, is what? Warding off the reflection of an intruder? A witless, blunted needle? Unable to consider a translucent solid without reticulate neuration? Blinker your eyes, reader, and peer inside. It is in the nature of my imagination to doubt itself – almost at once. What is the chief quality that separates me from a dragonfly? Apart from eye-size, brain-size, the power of flight, the spectacular colouring, my glass-clouding breath . . . I have some queasy consciousness of myself. Let me turn and look out from hide, hair and internal medicine from a point that seems to be about half an inch behind the dead-centre of my eyes.

Can dragonflies ever close theirs? I cannot wink mine. No sapajou, capuchin or white-face can. Possible, however, is a single, expressionless, shutting and opening of one eye.

What? A monkey that *speaks*? I appeal to your imagination – see gold-veined above.

Yes? Then what language is it? Come, I am sure the educated, occidental reader of this will have read versions of ancient Japanese pillow books. In the original he or she would be deaf and blind, is at the mercy and good faith of the translator. Naturally this is no criticism of the ancient Japanese with their white-painted faces and black-painted teeth and only reaffirms that what is expressed and how varies considerably across language.

Ah, but the reader would recognise script as script though not sure in which direction to follow it? I have not said monkeys can write or transcribe sounds into symbols. I am appealing to your belief in the oral tradition, transcripts and translations – but mostly I would point to a drawing of Japanese children catching dragonflies, a plaintive wail of '*ya-hor-ra ya-hor-ra ya-hor-ra*' attracting the male, while '*tombo*', also thrice, attracts the female. It is a system akin to vociferous fishing; a three-metre rod and a call naturally dependent on the sex of the bright bait attached to the metre-long line. Skill is needed to entice the dragonfly prey towards sticky bird lime or near enough to pounce upon.

Is there anything else before I begin the right-angled brackets? Yes, supplementary to the above: a few etching titles remain untranslated either because they are well-known words or because their meaning requires more length – such will be found in the body of the particular commentary.

And last, a vital physical note on our burly burin-wielder: he suffered a peculiar limitation which made his relation to my Duchess very quiet and almost speechless. He was deaf to the extent that his sense of hearing barely counted. He could hear no trickle of water, no whirr, no sticky flesh – and no voices. There were compensations; amongst them the summer crust and dust of what, in winter, is the light-headed salt air of Sanlúcar, the shift of sweat, the swollen fingertips, the eyes shying for shadows and the lips, licked, redundant in their usual muscles.

1

THE DUCHESS'S

CRAFT

———

EMBARCACION

DE LA DUQUESA

IN THE SECOND COURTYARD, THE ONE I NORMALLY
and formally lived in, was a raised stone tank, some
twenty-five feet by ten by two, in which there lived,
chiefly to keep down mosquitos, a few mottled fish.

On the day our artist arrived this was also occupied
by a water-sopping raft of bamboo and rope.

The view is not quite on the diagonal, is from nearly
a column along and two short strides out of the
cloister, with one of the four regularly placed palm
trees just out of sight to the right.

Reclining on the raft, on cushions, shaded by an
awning and aired by a punkah operated by her black,
white-dressed goddaughter, is the black-dressed
Duchess. The raft has a rug and some Turkish-style
brassware aft where the humans are and, everywhere,
a variety of wildlife; to wit, a tethered goat near the

prow, a small dog who has come forward to midships, an unconscious guacamayo on a perch by the tenting and a sapajou at the far, forward corner, wearing a harness and two butterfly wings of wire and buttercup yellow silk. Beside him, on the stone border, is an octagonal pewter plate containing dried fruit and nuts, mostly shelled almonds.

For some time previously the sapajou had been carefully examining a dusty walnut for the health of the fruit and to find the weak point in the meandrine shell. Found, the nut was cracked – to reveal a waving, greenish worm. In spite of his disgust, the sapajou wondered – doubtfully, by analogy, not colour – on peach-fed ham. It was at this point that he looked up and round at the noise of the artist's entry. I am not sure: even very close examination of my hands and walnut does not make clear if there is a waggle-cum-score for the worm.

The goat is chewing, lower jaw towards the artist, a few, messy strands of hay. That may be an added udder – to provide milk for the voyage. The guacamayo, in life arthritic-clawed and vicious-beaked, sits warming in the sun six months after dropping like a sad orange and going off to be plucked and salted and settled in pure alum solution, its beak to be touched up, its eyes to be buttoned. I mean the artist did not make the creature dead and preserved but cockatooed one eye, struck out the perch and had the bird grip the nearest awning pole the which, narrowing my eyes, is topped by a cast-iron crescent. The small dog, with its raisin-nose and tufts of curly white hair (ribbon forgotten or removed) looks dismayed and fragile-legged. Both humans appear alarmed, the reclining Duchess pleasurably so . . . the artist is about to pay his respects and will gladly leap on board to do so.

He jumped. The tank, not deep and with a fair amount of water displaced by the conceit, still had movement in it when eighty-odd kilos landed forward. The sapajou had already departed before boots hit bamboo, in three skips and a spring was up a vine-clad cloister column. He turned. The tilting guacamayo toppled. Pale almonds led a spray of brazils and wrinkled apricots. The dog burrowed into cushions, thrusting its wet nose between damask and rope. The goat bleated and the Duchess and punkah-wielder rose, one delighted, the other letting out a curt *mezzo-soprano* skirl.

The artist unhatted like a slave dealer and the sapajou – cha! – understood that his false wings had punctured and snagged.

The noises below reminded me of a bird, a swift I think, trapped in a room – breath and shrieks, frantic wings – here underlaid by the most sonorous of fish-stunning slops and then joined by a medley of watery bellows, slaps, rattles and twittering honks – some like a band of nose-flutes tuning up. Also a woody-leafed tremor. My wings were caught.

The goat disembarked, skidded and with touchy, old dignity looked around for something else to crop. The re-hatted artist helped the Duchess down. Something leafy and crushed, a miserable acidic and must perfume in my nostrils. I jiggled, gibbered – chipchipchip – and sneezed. My Duchess started, saw me, tented her nose with her hands. Then she brought them away as if both pointing me out and delightedly receiving applause.

Heads turned. The artist nodded. Of the simpler choices available – bending from the first storey, hoisting the Duchess to stand on his shoulders and clasping her ankles to his ears or even fishing me down with a pole from the collapsed awning – he took none. Instead, he stripped off his jacket, tossed it to the goddaughter and approached the column with a judicious weightlifter's roll.

I was privy to a peculiar though lid-cut perspective – a plumpish breast but under it a powerful belly and, even when not foreshortened, very stocky legs. His face turned up. His long nose, normally a whiffler, was here stiff with intent. One eye squint-closed on me, his lower teeth scraped twice on his upper lip. I was inverted over an intimidating, meaty gargoyle. His back humps. A stifled grunt of effort and muscle-strangled lungs. The vine shudders, his bushy hair shakes. I am intrigued by his large earlobes, pink and soft as a cow's teets, alarmed by the rigid, grimace-making neck tendons buoying them up.

My Duchess loves a show. Her hands cover her nose – for him this time – then come together, are squeezed between her knees, then clap-clap a summons to encouragement.

He rewards me with a terrific, long-toothed, silent snarl. His breathing – infrequent – is like another puncture. Neither he – nor I – trust the dry vine. He pauses, spits out dust and vegetable scurf. Behind him the goddaughter, still with his jacket, righted the guacamayo and dechted its beak.

I jigged perfunctorily. He fought gravity with bolted horse-rider's thighs, heels and hands, knuckles and fingertips white, the rest piebald with patches and spots of red, while his belly and shoulders did the hefting. Perhaps he nearly swooned. In his alarmed, sweating, fifty-year-old vanity he must have thought I was constructed like a cat, with ample skin at the neck. Or perhaps he thought I was about to escape and leave him where he was, all public exhibition and no pet. With a sound like the gruffest of appeals he reached up, grabbed me and tore. The wing wire stretched and stretched more – but it was the vine that cracked. As soon as it had, he dropped me. In a moment I had touched ground and sprung, tail whirling, punctured silks rattling, to clasp my Duchess's bosom. My lids felt blind tight, my throat throttled, my armpits raw. Everyone was delighted; applause pattered, I was kissed and petted, various hands plucked bits of twig and vineleaf from my fur, others pointed out my bedraggled silks and one elongated wing. The trembling artist brushed himself down. His trembling was different from mine; a waistcoated gorilla with a galloping pulse and twitching muscles, he sniffed and smirked. My thirty-four-year-old Duchess shyly offered her reversed hand by way of thanks, while stroking me with the other. Slowly fixing a kiss on to her knuckles, the artist looked up and eyed me, his expression a replete mix of bonelessness and cupidity. This changed. Abruptly and absurdly his eyes smarted, as if my Duchess's hand could reek of onion.

2

THE DUCHESS'S

GUEST

———

HUESPED

DE LA DUQUESA

TO THE RIGHT, A SOLDIER-CARDINAL'S CAMPAIGN
bed rescued from a storeroom, brought along and set
up for her guest. Perched on the baldaquin a white-
face monkey is carefully shelling a shrimp. Or perhaps
just peering at it. The light is bad, making the bed-
drapes black not red, and reducing the capuchin to a
tailed shape with knuckles and, rough sculpted in
greyish putty, an old man's face; he is Socratic, white-
whiskered, with an unlikely but accurate streak of
black fur worn straight back off the balding forehead.

The back wall has already been marked by charcoal.
It is difficult to say what is going to follow. There
appears to be some sort of plimsoll line. That mark in
the far corner may be the beginnings of a post, that
other one, the head of a drowning dog. The effect is
something of a visual quicksand. Is there a hint of

Venice? With no gondoliers, no gilt, no twists, no rope?

Centrally placed in a high-backed oval bath, steering a line to the post corner, the artist sits in a candled hat, sombrero below, candelabra above. His look and expression, some dry slits and flat dabs, are directed towards the viewer-door over a beefy (in life hair-fringed) shoulder. Is the shoulder wet? Or lit from another source? Those are melodramatic candles; lime-leafed, huge, they do not actually cast much light. Beside him, on a little table – the bag of bran is in the bath – is a large sponge in a dish. Barely visible on the bed is a jacket sleeve guillotined by the edge of the etching. He has removed all traces of the window to the right.

From my point of view let me mention that the shrimp had already been be-headed, de-legged and untailed. I was left with the clean little morsel and my shelling was confined to the back scales – more grey than pink in that light. Milky bran and shrimp – an interesting combination of smells, the latter sea salt, firm and sweet. I bit, chewed, swallowed. Below, water swirled as he rinsed. The artist got out, all dripping bran bag and juddering candle-flames, to reach for the towels. From my angle I could see some of my reflection in the puddle he left on the floor and work my tail in it. So.

Our artist enjoyed a suite of three interconnected rooms on the first floor on the north side of the third courtyard. The rooms marched westwards towards the already-mentioned second courtyard: the first a bedroom, the second housing ink and oils, the third set aside for the engravings. My Duchess let him choose place and furnishings, the latter a job he enjoyed at his leisure, beginning with bed and bath, a chair or two, but going on for almost a fortnight, often picking things in poor condition – a woodwormed bench, a crippled console – or indulging a taste for bizarre knickknackery and juxtaposition. A sheep's skull, which from some angles looked like an extravagant, bauchled shoe, he placed on the seat of a gilt brocade armchair that was losing its stuffing; with her permission he teased horsehair up to eye sockets and out of nasal holes and ear, to make a ginger and bleached-bone dragonsheep. She did smile but quickly moved on to see and smell his artists' materials.

In the second or middle room he had his easels and some tables and, to the smell of pasty pigment or fusty blank ink, he painted, drew or wrote his letters. Like the bedroom this one had a door to the outside. The third or last room was little more than a cube cave. In terms of copper plates the whole series of forty-two was laid end to end around it with two doorways, one genuine, left over. He placed each plate on the floor to lean against the wall like a half cloche or a tilted-copper skirting board. He started at the farthest corner to the right from the door, came back towards the entrance, jumped it and went round. The only window, high and as small as an absent stone block, he anyway kept shuttered; the room was always dark and he always worked by candle. Incidentally, he laid out those plates *before* they were marked, sat in the doorway with the engraving tools behind him, usually worked using his crossed left knee as support, would often get up to walk in the etchings room and consider. He was thus always working to a fixed number of plates and left gaps. I know – from under his chair – that he did. Also that he marked the false door – not much more than a charcoal jamb – between the end of the series and the beginning. There was never any idea that the series should be circular and the charcoal lines – that false door was a deliberate cut – did not obey the same dog-brisk instincts that led him to mark the bedroom. He worked directly on the plates. The second room, in a band from the height of his hip to the top of his head, became a maze of preparatory drawings of her hands and fingers, the shape of her head and hair, the hang and fold of certain materials on her body but all in a mix of scales so that an eyelid was larger than a small figure, a hand huge beside a chin.

3

THE DUCHESS'S

PICTURE GALLERY

———

PINACOTECA

DE LA DUQUESA

A MISNOMER. THE VIEW IS ALONG A CLOISTER — the one in the background of the first engraving, behind the raft and palms. A small, wing-crippled sapajou is portrayed at the right, lower foreground where the flag-stoned floor meets the low wall at the beginning of the latter's journey across the metal.

The artist has removed the trio of paintings on the inner wall above the walnut table — two yellow and orange pumpkin '*bodegones*' flanking a fanciful masque with swans and goddesses — and replaced them with one painting taken from elsewhere, possibly from the real gallery — upstairs, running through two courtyards — possibly with a painting of his own. Angle and varnish make it difficult to be certain but it is definitely the portrait of a person — there is that hood-like look round the face and the flesh looks tessellated from forehead to cheekbone, becomes ragged towards the chin. I am not sure why I have thought of the pallid, late Duke – after all, it is not possible to see and would be an abeyance of taste so soon after his death. I think it must be the depth of the black in the hood; it would make cowl enough for a monk.

The two persons considering the work are the artist and the ducal widow. He is hatted again (though only for the etching) and, almost in profile, is bending a little backwards, belly out. A sardonic pout is that? Or a cigar smoker's? She has arranged her feet as for a formal pose, heel to instep and her body is full to the viewer. Note the fan – real silver and black silk, the silver honeycombed like a brandysnap – which, slightly off-handedly, indicates the portrait on the wall. As well as shoes he has given her a black lace mantilla raised in two places. Her expression is remarkable, looks brief, as if she were simply checking the painting was still there and waiting to move on to the next.

What else? Outside the engraving the spy wore no wings. Neither did she. In point of fact these stances came before his bath and my baldaquin shrimp. For forty-eight hours so did the etching but then he decided on intercalated sop to travel and hygiene. It also occurs to me that he may first have had this title in mind for the whole series but left it for one. Ironic sometimes but never an ironist. She had no fan. They strolled post-raft, she delighted with his deafness, he affable but thirsty. He seemed pleased by the swans pulling a chariot-cum-boat and amused by the puffed cheeks of the trumpeter in *The Triumph of Summer* but, freed of my wings by the goddaughter, I scooted closer to make sure. His lips twitched – some pressure on lip liquid made the movement begin with a small, sticky crack. Gum on paper. A mistake in gumming corrected – to get the sheets properly lined up. It was her nerves that surprised me, her hair-tugging, lace-twitching fingers – and her dusty feet as if she had worked her toes in dry clay. His thumb dab-wiped the corners of his mouth. She kept her eyes on him, he considered a swan. From my angle – consider, by his boots, his britches – a low, bi-globular upward turn, a mild swelling of the Leda bend above. The parched tenderness, the ache and tremble were in her throat. Was he embarrassed? More bemused. The jacket over his arm moved over his belly while the fingers of his other hand began to fiddle with the hair in his ear, roll it like a waxed moustache. I had never seen her expression before – eyebrows a T cap for the nose, mouth tiny, eyes anxious, wrinkles crêpe thin. A hint I thought, in her barely-lifted chin, of her sniffing him. Something lubricated, warm, bland. I sneezed. She smiled distractedly and in the movement from *The Triumph of Summer* to an overblown still-life he shifted as if cheerfully uprooting his feet. Relief? No. In a sudden burst, the zest of decision, she thrust her arm under his at the elbow, almost closed one eye on him and half-stumbled, half-leant against him.

4

THE MENAGERIE

IS ALL EUPHORIC, ANIMALISTIC FLOURISH. AN ideal semicircle, it consists of a peacock in the centre, its enlightened tail erect, using, if you look with attention, a large tortoise as a pedestal and, pairing outwards on either side of the curve under gouts of tail-induced radiation, a lynx and a badger, a crane and a fantastic flamingo, a goat and a deerhound from the same place as the flamingo.

The tortoise is starred, overshadowed and has its head obscured by the small white dog, although, judging by the fudge and dark where the stubby, grey feet should be, the artist may have had the reptile withdraw or simply excluded the contents of the carapace.

I am not sure whether my role – in the foreground, head to one side, wearing a fez with an inapposite tassel hanging down like a plumbline, crouching with one hand raised – is that of a left-handed orchestra conductor or not. In any case, what kind of noise would this chorus make? Or was that not his responsibility? His deafness had two aspects; not only did he ignore sounds around him but his disregard for the sounds *he* made was as startling and indiscreet as an unoiled oarlock.

What have we then? An offering to her? An ingratiating arrangement? Something sentimental? And if it is some kind of private talk, what would a deerhound mean?

Stop – these are not pictorial concepts. But I do mean that at one time I should have been, was, one eye cocked, very wary of this impossible grouping, so plume perfect, all ridiculously together . . . until a certain sullenness came out and some tiny strokes at the eyes, at the corner of suitable mouths, led to a green and melted butter leer for some of them.

The crane is looking off, the flamingo may be drinking, gobble and gravity, the badger is about to swing away and that small dog – still on, or re-membering, the raft – is barely a second before alarmed retreat or rushing forward to nip an ankle.

This engraving is probably the best-travelled on its wall. Origin-ally fourth, it became second after the raft, third after the bath, jumped to sixth and even got as far as twelfth before having its speckling of dried lime-wash wiped on his shirtsleeve and returned to where it started; he had a complacent, almost pessimistic respect for his original notions.

And *that* selection? She had quite a number of other unsuitable animals for him to choose from. I can understand why he ignored the occupants of the kitchen courtyard, a pack of dull-coloured mutts and brutes in a dun desert. Or even the solitary occupant of the formal, small-hedged, stone-boxed courtyard with its statue of a young boy offering up a clam shell and with a rank beanstalk twining up his right leg and flowering modestly over his thighs, though the studded hood the hawk wore and the remains of chicken heads about it made for a striking contrast. But I am uncertain as to why he should exclude other sharers of the diseased orange tree rectangle and separate the badger, lynx and crane from the guineafowl, an ermine and a bulldog. The crane, a hunting casualty, with an ill-healed and incomplete wing, ruled over a smelly, caged truce. The guineafowl pecked about and the bulldog, a stentorious, timid creature, often waited for the nocturnal badger outside its cage, while the lynx paced and the ermine had fits of writhing and scuffing, made thudding circuits of its wood, wired box. And from my courtyard he has excluded the Egyptian cat – the only other animal there able to use vines and columns as a route to the roof. The peacock was shabby and impotent. And had a wife.

You may like to compare the light effects of the menagerie with those of the bath, the candled hat shining up, the bright fowl round and down. The comparison bothers me but I am not sure whether that is due to my very suggestible harking for water, stars and dark, slow shapes beneath, or to something unconscious or routine in his division of the plates. Even if I make a great effort and superimpose one set of scratches on the other there are still too many flecks and lashes to be sure of an eye, too much striated light to be sure of a passage or a tunnel. Coincidence? No. The carapace and the bath are not quite aligned.

23

5

A Duchess's
Supper

Cena
de una Duquesa

Why 'a' duchess sometimes and 'the' at others? Unsure of his articles? Well, this is not the only supper portrayed in the series but is the gorged first. Although there were many others at the table – there always were – he has limited the persons portrayed to just two. My Duchess is laughing at the person out of frame to her right, her chin back almost on her shoulder, her throat splendidly illuminated. Her dress is white lace and she has a single ribbon hanging down between left cheek and ear, a silk ringlet. Our artist, hatted again like a traveller, his face slyly shadowed again, is putting out his hand to take a sea-urchin which he will divide and eat, after squeezing on to the innards a drop or two of lemon juice from one of the quarters shown, raw.

On an oval silver ashette there are fat prawns. Some

gaping mussels in a hot sauce are in a round dish. There are fingerbowls and bowls of mayonnaise and aioli and something pepperish (red like the prawns and the hot sauce, here seething shades of grey); there will be fish (*urta*) baked in a case of salt, the crust cracked, the fish removed and, its juices all retained, quickly filleted and served; and there will be beef so rare the laundrymaids will complain of the blood on the napkins. There are wineglasses, their contents, manzanilla and one from the Loire, carefully distinguished, not just by the curve of the glasses, but by the palest of tones.

It is a *crowded* table. In the lower foreground is a sapajou, portrayed as rather smaller than real and with something about him of the bushbaby, modestly hunched and concentrating on eating what looks like the meat of a small crab's claw.

I would particularly draw attention to the light again; my Duchess is in a beam of light as there is in a painting of an ecstatic nun in what was the Duke's bedroom, though she has a patch of grease on her cheek. And the artist's shoulders are burly enough to make him neckless. His face, brim-shadowed, is also foreshortened so that mouth and nose are very close together. His extended hand, almost fingerless to the viewer's eye, dense as a knuckle-rap, looks like a paw over the spiky sea-fruit.

6

THE HOWDAH

———

EL CASTILLO

SHOWS A LARGE, STARRED TORTOISE ROCKING and plodding leftwards. Attached to its back by means of a wide leather belt is a wooden box in which sits a capuchin monkey wearing not a jewelled turban or even a jockey's cap on its head but a pair of what look like bluebottle wings on its back. The monkey carries in one hand a long, thin stick, a budded switch, that reaches down to the ground where it has left an unbroken but seismocopic trail in the thickish dust.

The belt is carefully done, with its buckle and holes, looks almost as old as the reptile, though rather drier and more worn. The wings have no harness and no outer wires. The tortoise-elephant is almost in profile, its wrinkled neck eagerly outstretched. The capuchin-maharajah looks squeamish from the lurching, watches the viewer, has his right hand clutching the decoration on top of the box corner – one of four acorns. A jardinière?

Cube and hump absurdity? Yes. Humorous? Yes. The tortoise was never saddled for transport and I was never encouraged to ride it or even to sit on it, particularly when it had just been oiled. As is usual with tortoises the creature had minimal energy or wit but was as long-lived – maybe even longer – than the guacamayo. In the breeding season it was a little more active and would clash its shell against stones and heave at the base of vine-free columns. I once pointed out a large parasite in its tail. I would occasionally feed it fruit – not by hand, those jaws could crush small fingers and to be cornered by that broadside shell bears no thinking about – and watch it, for scientific purposes, lumber after a wild strawberry that I would, with a stick, tack in the dust. The creature's enthusiasm did not dim as the fruit became coated and dull and lost shape. It would eat pulp and grit with undiminished, dribbling delight.

That was in June, a month before the artist came. Perhaps my Duchess told him. Perhaps the stick was his own idea. There is no sign of a strawberry.

I am unable to help the reader as to *why* he chose to order his work as here represented or why he dithered and frowned so much, so early. Luxuriating in choice? Possible. I do know, however, that the next three plates changed order so often and sometimes so quickly that I can no longer remember all the moves and when they were made, only that he tried out every permutation – except *Twice Said* now – at least once. Let's see. *Housekeeper, Twice Said, Goddaughter; Goddaughter, Twice Said, Housekeeper; Goddaughter, Housekeeper, Twice Said.* And the present arrangement. It seemed more. But does this really matter? It is not, after all, as if this were a novel told in engravings on copper pages. That would be a contradiction in terms, surely, like a statue that indulged in stiff grimaces and blinks.

He had an odd habit of shutting his eyes and turning his face up and round as if to a brisk, miniature sun. Did he sometimes try to listen? Or perhaps he was merely shutting his eyes to open them afresh. Whatever the cause, he proceeded to depict persons round my Duchess but excluded from round her table all males, including her factor, her steward, her secretary, and most females, even those in her train like her personal maid and her private cook. He limited himself to accomplices, choosing

7

THE HOUSEKEEPER

EL AMA DE LLAVES

AND PORTRAYING HER STANDING SELF-CONSCIOUSLY and ingratiatingly beside a half-open bedroom door through which most of a capuchin monkey has gone, leaving visible only the hindquarters and tail, rather cattish at first glance but not when you consider the length and form of the raised tail and the shape of the heels and the existence of toes. There is nothing to indicate the housekeeper's post and her loyalties – no collection of keys, no mistress's ring. This is just a dumpy, toothless old woman dressed like a baker's wife with an arrangement round her head framing her face between clout and nunnish wimple. Her face lacks bones, is lumps of moistish flesh underbuoyed by soft jowls. Her lips – that is a sort of smile – are barely visible and where visible cracked and ragged. Her eyebrows are sparse, a few greased pig's bristles, her eyes dark, small and wet. He has managed her pallor with remarkable accuracy and also, as it were, the declining density of her face; those jowls look as light as the egg-based desserts she liked the which, along with soft caramel and violet comfits, were brought to her by Chechu, the gardener's feeble-minded boy.

She was more caretaker than housekeeper since my Duchess was not even an annual visitor, the *palacete* was almost always shut up – though opened serially and circuitously, courtyard by courtyard, as it was cleaned by the other permanent servants. These were all women. The only men who regularly entered – the estate office and factor were outside – were the gardener and his son, the boy responsible for feeding and watering the menagerie. Chechu was a dull, hunched soul with fuzz on his cheeks, most impressed by the hawk, most alarmed by the ermine – even when the crane was skinning his knuckles – and the housekeeper usually treated him with nods and smiles and chivvying, conspiratorial pats. Though I remember at least one occasion – I think I had something to do with it – on which her voice became like a shrill, frantic jew's harp and her slapping hand moved as fast as someone buffing a boot, while he, almost as fast, blinked and, a gasp slower, stuttered and twitched. She was a considerable seamstress. She had a habit, particularly when sat on the wooden chair that had an arm that folded up to bear her meal trays, of pressing the ball of her thumb into her nostril like some snufftakers. She, however, would merely separate the nostril vent, let it come together again, then part the flesh once more. She rang the bell every evening, a soft ritual clanking taken to each of the four courtyards, before sitting down to her supper.

When the owner was there excitement made her pallor take on patches of flush and old pore, made her manner a mix of eager complaisance and self-flattery. She called my Duchess '*mi niña*' (my girl), or, when remonstrating with her, '*chiquilla*' (lassie) – immediately dabbing out the sign of the cross on her chest as briskly as the cook brushed sugared water on bun dough, ending with her thumbnail to her lips and an aged simper. It was she who made my costumes but this had nothing properly to do with me. It was my Duchess she served and there were no stays to her devotion. She loved to see herself reflected in those personal belongings of my Duchess which were glazed or polished. I used sometimes to follow her to watch her chief, private pleasure. When she had made sure that the dinner table was correctly laid she would take a piece of muslin and rub and peer, rub and peer, at her Duchess's own set of knives, forks and spoons. The silver was old, heavy, over-ornate and never gleamed very much, but she – her eyesight was deteriorating – would hold up each item until it almost touched her cheek.

Incidentally, he excised the belt she always wore. It had a trio of keys on it, each with a separate clasp. The first of these was to the key box, a miniature commode with shallow drawers in which, on velvet, were the china key, the gold key, my Duchess's private cellar key and so on.

8

A GODDAUGHTER

———

UNA AHIJADA

MY DUCHESS HAD OVER ONE HUNDRED AND twenty godchildren but few of the others were black or half-adopted and none other was here included. She was about fifteen years old. He has sat her in a high-backed chair and dressed her well and fashionably. Sitting on her lap is a serious sapajou, also full-face. Despite a sort of whirlwind technique – close repeated curves, emphasised by the monkey's tail, long as a human arm, curled round her thigh – the effect is static and grave, her eyes browed and wary, the monkey prim and watchful. She is barefoot, her feet and knees tight together. Her right hand retains the monkey's waist. Both look – just fractionally – tired of posing.

We are an unlikely pair for any number of reasons. I never saw the girl sit like that. Though squattish she was not as plump nor as old as he has made her. She was a tagger, though always on the point of giving up, of sitting down, of complaining of fatigue. And she was frightened of and sometimes shrieked at live animals – she too much preferred the guacamayo stuffed. She would have shied away at any suggestion that I sit on her lap and would never have stayed still if I had dropped there. What she did adore, shoes, he has not given her. She was particularly fond of two pairs she had, both green – one lime, one mint. She disliked wearing them down but did not take them off to avoid doing that. She traipsed along in dresses gathered under her bust, with a light, fringed shawl over her shoulders and under her elbows, clutching the fringed ends in her hands. It gave her a bent-back look. Though her legs were sturdy, her walk was very soon, in ten or twenty paces, not far off a stumble. Her grip on her shawl made her progress even more laborious, yoked her on any stairs. Later she would sit, as if sounding her gloom and measuring her effort by the new scuffs and marks on her shoes and their relationship to the bunions and corns on her feet. Had I been the artist I might have put her in that position; sitting on a chair with one foot on one knee, her eyes on the foot, the shoe held by the heel, rhythmically tapping out a very picture of reluctance and regret.

What else of her impressed me? She had frequent eye problems and the brightness of the blood-shot whites, an orange in the inner eye like that of a limpet, was striking indeed. I suppose the colour of her skin, a peacock sheen on octopus ink, may have interested our artist for similar reasons – contrast and colour. That is, the technical novelty may have been more interesting to him than anything else.

In his freedom he certainly considered other possibilities; when squatting manfully, hand on one thigh, a small vinetwig in the other, he scratched and sketched out on the sandy ground a portrait of the goddaughter naked, first leaping, almost gnarled. With great speed and smacks of his hand to set the grains up, he righted and fleshed her, then twigged in my tail as if I were a clinging, furry undergarment and widened the black girl's eyes. I blinked. He smacked and rubbed, addressed himself to a re-smoothed patch. He wrote something on it (the date?), cleaned it, slowly, slowly shaded the earth-sand mix, cleared that, blew out and skilfully imitated the track of a snake. Cleared that with a tremendous smack of his beefy palm before giving in and getting off his hunkers and, face grimacing, stretching his legs, massaging a knee, scratching the back of his neck, grunting at me in a parody of rueful companionship. I do not know if his twig ties in with my mahout tortoise switch. He did, by the way, keep notebooks – surprisingly crude and thick brushstrokes, very deliberately done, invariably of figures, the pose, without detail.

9

TWICE SAID

DOS VECES DICHO

IS THE THIRD OF THIS MOST-SHUFFLED TRIO. THE
guacamayo holds the stage and struts in profile, beak
open, one leg goose-stepping, like some endlessly
didactic clockwork. The artist has made me an aged
schoolboy, with pince nez and a brimless little hat like a
soft lozenge. My head is cocked, I am listening with
great attention but while the bird seems triumphant in
his exposition, his pupil seems worried by the implica-
tions. My hat has been needle-worked; sprouted
orange seeds round the edge, a full orange in the centre.

I have tried hard to think why he might have been so
interested in re-animating that dumb corpse. Its colours
– red breast and head, blue and green wings – were not
transferable to copper and its curved beak, like a crab's
leading claw though a great deal quicker and more
precise in life, rarely opened as wide as he shows. He has
also made the bird shorter and more rounded than real
– the guacamayo was actually nearly twice my height.
And he was overfond of laconic titles.

Let me close my eyes a moment. Of course it is true that a monkey is able to mimic human expressions and gestures and that some birds are able to imitate human speech or at least some word sounds. (See Foreword.) The guacamayo could not. It could whistle and chuckle while feeding, a kind of self-encouragement and quite devoid of interest to others – the whistle had no intention, the chuckle no point. The chuckle was often accompanied by shelly cracks, the whistle, softer and fruitier, all to do with a sharp beak and a clear throat. It could also screech and caw. I do not know if anyone ever tried to teach the creature to say something and failed, or if it had forgotten. I have no idea how far along a lifespan of some one hundred and eighty years it was – only that it was ancient enough for aphasia and far older than the artist ever showed it. With stiff, scaly feet, an unkempt look and a greyish film on its eyes, it stank of evil temper. It only stirred for sudden, furious screeching, never threatened, always bit.

I must confess. Humour is absurd, fear illogical. But under-stand your commentator. *Once* may be the bright good-humour he blithely gave it. The trouble with my brain is that it has little science and none when asleep. Dream resurrected the creature at night, the stiff neck would ruffle, the eyes gleam. *Twice* may be my nightmare that just as smoothly ignored taxidermy. I'd find the forensic fowl with its claws dug into my chest about to make the first incision in my belly with its beak. I'd wake at this point to find my own hands clutching my chest, having plucked out my own soft hairs. I'd shudder. I would check both perch and shadow but would shudder again and have to spend time ridding myself of certain fears and images; something like a skinned rabbit hanging from a hook, silent, moonlit, garish flight and, worst of all, to a prior sound like hawking, the thud and sight of a roundish pellet of fur-stuck bones.

The French-made (in Lille) copper plates belonged to a scheme of the dead Duke to have the Coto Doñana portrayed by M. Guillaume du Sangé. I have some memory of this person – too many joints, an unusual cut and colour to his clothes – but not much. After only two or three excursions in the direction of the flamingo ponds he sickened. Malaria? If I ever knew I can no longer remember. Perhaps it was cholera.

'*Effrayeux, madame, effrayeux,*' he neighed to the house-keeper whenever she asked after his condition.

This is almost, but not quite, the only French I know. The poor fellow's neigh became whinny, his whinny throat-rattle and yellow, rolling eyes. Through window bars I watched them lay out his lanky corpse. And yes, despite his fine bones and elegant hands, he had, at least from my perspective, extraordinary toes, plump and rounded as shalottes on pegs – though the damp cloths did not swoop down to them or to the soles of his arch-fallen feet.

I never saw any of the sketches he made when out on horseback and do not know if the plan was purely topographical or also included flora and/or fauna. He certainly never sketched any of us. He brought with him a lot of clanking equipment – most of which returned north with his forgettable assistant. To which of them did the dry, sand-red hair belong? My memory here is wiggish. I know nothing of the contract, of the faint Duke's exigences or of M. du Sangé's working methods, except a thing like a sheet-music holder through which he squinted and with which he had some problem. I do not even know if he actually brought the plates, only that they were for his future use, which future truncated meant that they remained virgin for four years until my Duchess gave them to our artist when they were exploring the warehouse part of the palace, looking through storerooms, under dustsheets. They enjoyed dust on their relation, dust on his vein, dust on her hands, a kind of dry, mote and fust anointing. The copper had been carefully protected in oilskin and waxed paper and chamois leather and placed on a slate-topped console. She had him unwrap. Was he displeased? Unpleasantly surprised. He was a considerable miser with materials, seemed to resent too much. Here he examined a couple of the plates but mostly her for any flaws or offence. And in time terms *this* is the beginning of the series. Her offer was slowly accepted. He began by squeezing the ball of his thumb on the topmost copper surface of the stack as intently as the gardener affixing his print to a document. Tried severally for a clearer whorl, frowned, dabbed with a finger. He looked away, his eyes moving sluggishly from object to duty object: a marble bust, a walnut table, a rusted cast-iron candlestick. Finally, with more grunt than sigh, he pulled his hand up into his sleeve and rubbed, very gently at the marks he had made.

10

THE FARTHINGALE

EL GUARDAINFANTE

IS AN ARRANGEMENT OF THIN HOOPS AND THINNER
bars, like the rickety skeleton of a beehive kiln rather
than the cage it first resembles. It is topped by what
looks like a circular barber's strop, a ring of padded
blue-black leather, which is hinged to allow entry
from the back. The contraption sits on the floor, does
not ride on dummy's hips; the vaulted storeroom is
not a museum. There is no dress to drop down and
swell out over it.

On the barber's waistband is perched a preening
guacamayo, its neck bent, beak open, keeping its
claws clean and sharp-pointed.

Lower down, centrally placed, with its tail curled
round a vertical bar, a sapajou sits hunched over
another tidbit – in this case a lip-shelled pistachio.

It is one of the simplest of the etchings, almost
entirely linear but for fur and feathers. There are no
shadows, only a brisk corner. There is no hint of the
flagstone floor or of a light source or of the very pretty
ribbed sections of the ceiling.

I really do not think it is meant to be some jocular re-run on vanity, talking women and the furry nature and place of their brains; his deaf clowning was altogether sharper and more twisted. That pistachio is too carefully lipped, that jutting neck feather too precise to be other than a scrupulous sort of tenderness, but above all the lines of hoops and bars are too carefully differentiated. Yes, and there was one link missing, there at the right where the hoop of the farthingale has sprung – which was, if I remember, the topographer's problem; a worn metal thread.

11

THE SEAMSTRESS

———

LA MODISTA

I AM NOT SURE I UNDERSTAND THIS TITLE. IT seems straightforward but it is not clear to me who the seamstress might be. It is just possible he could not remember the word he wanted and that this is a quirky mnemonic in a private thesaurus. Seems unlikely.

The plate shows a capuchin monkey (*Cebus capucinus*) in a scaled-down version of a flounced dress. Around the stamen-waist are arranged six stiffish petals, from which slightly thinner material hangs directly to the ground. The neck is lowish and trimmed, the sleeves to the forearm are puff-petalled. Likewise in petals the parasol. The hat has something piratical about it, though I am not busty, being plumed and with one side raised.

The expression of the capuchin is haughty. His feet are not visible, the tip of his tail is.

But do seamstresses ever dress like this? As an advertisement? A sampler of their skill? Or is there some third party involved? Who? Why so coy? Why so little faith in his titles?

The link with the previous etching and the previous century is clear though not, particularly at the sleeves, pure. I am not – the dress was dropped over my head, the hoops covered – an expert in changing fashions. My condition as a male, my fur, that hat – I can think of any number of reasons that might hinder my appreciation. And how uncomfortable the wretched cloth was, how heavy! It had none of the lightness of my first wings though of the same yellow silk, no breezy thrum and tug but tail-drowning flounces and suffocating weave. I had, with my non-parasol hand, to raise the dress to be able to walk.

My Duchess almost choked with laughter, rocked on her four-legged chair, stamped her feet. She made faces at me, blowing out her cheeks, plucking at her chin, frowning and pointing. An imitation? Not of me. I have hairs on my chin but not so singular.

The housekeeper trembled and shook – her first escaping laugh was a whoop. She clapped her hand to her mouth and from there, after a jerk and a fart like a cat's enquiring miaow, came irregular but powerful blasts of grass-blowing interrupted by skirling snorts.

And our artist? He observed with good-natured detachment the signs of their enjoyment; he smiled, watched my Duchess clasp and squeeze her housekeeper's hand, the tears on her cheeks, her delighted wince as her ribs hurt, the forward push of her feet as she twitch-lay back. He himself laughed only once – a decorous baritone guffaw – when the champagne cork wires that held up the parasol gave way and the material closed above my head.

And I am not sure. Did he put his ear to her chest? Was I jealous? Jealous enough to imagine it between indignantly ignorant blinks? Had he leant over? What was I jealous of? A woman is never as soft as her breasts. I yanked off the hat myself, dropped it and the parasol to the ground and then held up my flounces in mute appeal: take this off me.

But he had not finished with costume work. 'Stay still,' said the housekeeper. I thought the next might at least be more comfortable, suit my mood better, but he had me down for the clergy. Called

12

AND THE RED

Y EL ROJO

THE CLOTH WAS PUFFY MANDRILL PURPLE AND I was dressed as a sateen Monsignor White-face, not as the elegantly tailored Cardinal Sapajú in the engraving. That cummerbund – watered silk is that? – gleams more and the skirts are much stiffer than the hastily tacked outfit I wore. Those elegant cloth-covered buttons too are an addition and the snug skullcap kept slipping. Those splendid slippers I never wore. But at least there was (unseen) a welcome hole for my (unseen) tail; a recondite art critic with a taste for the mildly prehensile could do a monograph on his use of mine.

The expression given me is one of hierarchical gravity and compassion. My hands, joined at the fingertips and thumbtips, bespeak a proximate homily. But on what subject? The difference between sport and disport? Forms of entertainment and marriage?

There were three persons facing me. My Duchess had a bridesmaid – her goddaughter. She herself sat primly with a small posy of flowers in her lap. The artist sat beefily at his ease, leaning back, one leg forward. Out in the courtyard, blue sky, not church rafters.

Being a parody of a princely celibate does not make a monkey a moral taxonomist and I wonder if, apart from the rub of my Monsignor's habit, you can understand my discomfort, stymied and frantic, at being brought before these fantastic and extravagant people.

I am a tree-top trooper, here grounded, alone and in disguise. I sneezed helpless disapproval. But what was I to do? Sneeze again? I did. I had no host, no missal, no dogma, no ritual. The sun made my eyes water. Why did they want ceremony and theatre? A dark corner would have done. And what was I, an unusually dressed, unusual pet, supposed to be proving?

My Duchess smiled, placed her hand on his inner thigh. That woman had no sense of responsibility. No, no, she did, she did, was a champion of aristocratic privacy and impulse, had her own walls for her flight from convention.

In my confusion and unhappiness I found that I had raised my skirts and begun to play with myself. Had they given me a gold ring I should certainly have had congress with it. They had instead preferred a stalk of grass plucked from the bouquet, tied round her middle finger, the bridesmaid providing an index tip, the artist's clumsy stiff digits attending to and waggling about the bow.

'Yes, I do,' said my Duchess, jumping to her feet, clapping her hands, starting to applaud.

I turned my back on her – for that was where the buttons were.

A while after – delicately waiting till the *albero* soil had received a sprinkling of moisture and jelly – a female hand, smelling of salt and sap, stroked the fur on my head.

'*Ay, principe!*' said my sentimentally-wed Duchess, '*Ce truc-là est bien malin, n'est-ce pas?*'

Easy for her in her compassionate, we prisoners' voice. Where was my reward, my retort?

And yet, in spite of this, our artist was quite able to suggest, nesting me down, tracing me out in the plates, all over the plates, on the plates that I was some sort of mundane miracle, an amazingly swack escape artist to whom discomfort was quite foreign. There is a species of biting fly here that look like winged black commas. The problem is that they fly silently and their insulting slowness is due, in part, to the weight of your blood they have already sucked in. You blink, the comma gains height – and that is not a coincidental itch on your back but a bite. There is time enough for an exasperating choice: scratch and kill or vice versa. Take the second, see the trace of red on your palm – and almost at once, coming round your elbow, drifts another bloated punctum. It does not, incidentally, like any sort of wind, preferring still days to the *poniente* (the west wind) or the *levante* (the east), and particularly those days with a seeping mist in which the oyster-stone walls exude their origin in salt-weed smells.

Our artist, having had me impersonate a lady and a Monsignor,
decided now to show me in my natural dress in

13

MÁS EL LEVANTE

a title as gratuitous as the *levante* itself, a hot, dry, door-
juddering, ear-buffeting, dust-charged, eye-smarting wind
that takes three days from the first ominous tugs through the
howling to its wispy end. It is the howling that is much the
greater part, feels endless; the tugs and eddies are quite brief.
Más means more, in addition. It begins and dies quickly, but the
death is rarely noted, just the relief. You can feel the wind drying
the air, the moisture vanishing from the ground. Between your
fingers, between your toes, in all the joints and folds of your
carcase, sweat springs and forms and trickles. Windows have to
be shut: locks rattle, panes squeal, putty falls, dust dances. I
cannot think of a creature that gets benefit of it. My Duchess
dabs so at her lids that they become sore. It is a lovely detail.
Doors and windows are blocked with damp towels, she often
sits in a circle of women bathing her eyes in cold camomile tea;
wet eyes, tinctured lids.

Our artist used the dust-shrouded days to work hard. We may
even say that he put down the first structure of the series

courtesy of the *levante*, though he wiped and glowered and sweat, paps dripping, nose too, his shirt-back patching like the section through a mushroom. It is weather for stoics and suicides. He kept inside. For the etching however – ¡*tan pancho*! – he put us out.

THE WIND IS PULLING AND STRETCHING EVERY-thing towards the horizontal, towards the left. The palms in my courtyard are bending. The tortoise has shut up. The peacock and peahen huddle, ruffled. The blinded goat braves the wind. The cat tries to lie in the shelter of the watertank. And in all these animals the wind is shown as erasing their features and markings.

Only one creature looks unconcerned and is portrayed in sharp, hairy detail. Yes, my image has found a dead point, an eye of calm in the whirling dust behind one of the columns. Absurd, there was none. But there I am sitting with one leg stretched out, a gesture more human than simian, peeling a nectarine – perhaps a peach – at any rate the kind of grit-attracting fruit only a sot would try to eat in a *levante*.

The point? The joke of an animal unaffected by a circumstance that flattens and blurs all others? I do not know.

I will add that the *levante* sometimes blows up again – those wisps become tugs – for another three days and if very violent, beaches tons of unmoored seaweed that dries and stinks and becomes a mountainous fringe of fly-ridden black on the sand.

In most cases however, and this was one, the wind has cleansing effects, leaves the seawater clear and, sometimes, leaves interesting structures for people to find and explore.

14

THE DUNE POOL

ESTANQUE EN LAS DUNAS

The reader will have noticed, I trust, that so far all the etchings have been contained by walls and courtyards and that my Duchess, his correspondent, has as yet, hardly appeared – apart from that first smile under the awning about the size of a small fish, as a picture fancier, and then as an exultant diner.

That is about to change. But discreetly does it. An expedition was made. Let's see; three humans and three animals, a man and two women, one black, one white, a she-ass, a male sapajou and a small, curly white terrier left the little palace and, a mile along the dunes – some seabirds, mostly white with black heads to our left nearer the sea – we came across a miniature imitation of a valley and lake.

Now the water was not particularly deep – not nearly as deep as he was to make it – but was clearer than the air and showed the sand under it in a wonderful serpentine pattern. No small fish or crustacean had been trapped there as in a rock pool – there was, that is, nothing to detract from the clarity of the water and the grains of sand so expertly and sharply sculpted.

I was considering – how had this been done? What had contrived such a regular pattern? – when the canine raisin and curl began to yap with that tearful sound the very ineffectual use when they are frightened by the unfamiliar. I turned in time to see my Duchess and her goddaughter, their clothes discarded, about to step into the sand valley pool.

AND IT WAS THEIR BATH IN THIS BRIEF NATURAL accident that our artist delicately portrayed. He briskly flattened the peaks of sand and increased the depth of the water from calf to knee. Technically, the thing is a marvel. Splashing water must be hideously difficult to represent in an etching; that fabric of drops! And just how, in drops and grains, did he get sand to look dry and water to look wet?

On reflection: these playful women have been wrapped in veils, had a net thrown over them. They are all roundnesses – but with the discretion of mist and the tuck of pumpkins. Their slight crouch, to reach and push the tepid water, obscures. They do not even have navels.

This is quite a contrast to the gooseflesh, discoloured patches of skin, tight-centred breasts and dripping tufts in the pool I saw. Indeed, the goddaughter's modesty and dislike of cold meant the game was, at least at first, rather one-sided.

A few yards off our fully-clothed artist held the bridle, side-kicked sand at the excited, trembling dog to get it – successfully – to shut up and took in the scene.

In the etching I am portrayed accurately enough as sitting on a bank in a mournful posture, watching the two naked women. My cheek is on my hand; I could be suffering from toothache. In fact I am watching the sand pattern being destroyed by their feet, the water cloud in terribly slow explosions, the water clear as the grains sink to form a non-descript basin. My Duchess looked back. Her eyes were the colour of quicksilver. The goddaughter was cheering up by the moment and was about to start using one arm as a windmill – the spray would send me skelping down the reverse slope of the dune.

Our artist was fond of surprising angles, upturned women – and of certain forms of waiting. That was a morning expedition. Naturally. No one wished to burn. He waited some hours then, through a long mealtime, to the hottest, stillest time of day and

15

LA SIESTA

PILLOWS AND SHADOWS AND SHEETS FIRST MIS-
lead the eye into abstract slopes, fortuitous crevices.
But there it is – a view from a bedhead corner, my
Duchess and her goddaughter sprawled in clothed,
sisterly sleep.

Was that a sigh? The siesta breathes languor, a
thick-sprung parody of the raft, some Turkished.
Everything looks lightly dusted in sherbet. The etching
is a dream but in technique not that different from
dune sand and water, points rather than scratches,
dots rather than lines. The bed is impossible, too
rounded, too firm. My Duchess did have a chaise-
longue – for reading, not naps – and always took off
her clothes before getting into bed. I never saw her lie
down with another woman, clothed or not.

And yet, there she is, beside a buxomed black girl,
the upper sheet at knee-height for her, nearly waist-
high for the other. They are not intertwined. He has,
rather, set up a relationship of curves and swells and
cloth and has *exactly* rendered my Duchess's manner
and posture of sleep a turn before waking; the view is
over her black hair, her head to the right, her

shoulderblades touching the bed, though the right barely – the twist turns through her waist to her hips, left down, right above, her knees lifted, left slightly advanced and a pleasing (though here sheet-covered) fit of the toes of her right foot in the instep of her left. The goddaughter is less clearly realised or, perhaps, is meant only as shadow and relief for the godmother. Besides I can barely recall what she looked like at the same stage; smothered out by an impression of a jealous or sulkily possessive sleeper. It was my Duchess I knew. He has the quality of her sleeping skin on copper, grain and membrane, pearl and pallor – though I have always preferred to watch the morning sun on her flesh. She has one of those faces that is recomposed on waking. Sleep blurs it, flattens it off. Some faces, that is, show no change – he, sat in his waistcoat on a straightbacked chair, sleep squeezing out his jowls, is always self-possessed. In sleep, she is a kind of discomposition.

This is most striking in the face but is there in the naked body as well. Daily she wakes from the feet up, through calf, thigh, then gluteally. She stirs and turns, headwise on her side. Her breasts change, become conical, the pellet, settled down in the depression, a soft circle cup, falls out and, as slow as a snail, fills and tightens. That little wrinkled sweetmeat. The temptation to bite! I never did dare. A meditation on the nipple? Hardly. Still I have thought of a raisin on rice and cream. A light sprinkling of cinnamon. Too sweet? Too gelatinous?

Let us return then to bodies and bedding in which everything is pure white and shade, from sheets to dresses – and a saucer – its roundness is one of the initial misleading elements – which is not on the bed, but on the floor past her hair by the drooping sheet. It contains something oval and sticky. A slice of prickly pear?

This is also the etching in which I least appear – I am little more than a white-faced profile about to lap with something like the tip of a cat-tongue brush. That may be milk about the pear.

A short admission. I have looked back on the account so far. Failings? Some white-face clumsiness in the structure and handling of a sentence or two. Perhaps also a certain abruptness of movement. But these are trifles only. What made me turn and look was the fear that I might have botched my memory, missed an entire element, misunderstood the nature of his scratches, seen an eye but overlooked the peacock's tail or found fur in a patch of dust.

But then I reminded myself that the affair had something in it of blunt, vigorous mime – remember, reader, to cut out the sound not just of water but of his fricative caress – and I concentrate again on watching her thigh flesh pucker the semi-moon traces on her skin, and compare with the corresponding scratches his hand and burin made on copper.

But let us put this in perspective. Here follows a note on the words used on me, the vocabulary often exclamatory, the questions rhetorical, the use of diminutives extensive. There is even an alphabetical vowel slide from endearment to reproach.

¡Ah, mi niño!
¡Eeh, que cosita!
¡Ay, amorcito!
¡Oh, cabroncete!
¡Uh, guarro!

I find men rarely address me. Women, who may or may not be nervous of my teeth, seem often to be half-speaking to themselves, smile and look hurt in equal proportions. The following is an almost inclusive summary of the words I hear:

'*¡Carita, carita blanca! ¿Dónde estas? ¡Ven, ven! ¡Amorcito! ¡Oye! Pero ¿ qué haces? ¡Quieto! ¡Toma! ¡Bicho malo! ¡Fuera! ¡Guarro! Bueeeno, toma. Chúpate algo más sano. ¿Quieres fruta? ¡Mira que fruta! Deja eso. Venga, sé buen chico.*'

Which translates more or less as follows:

'Facie, white-facie! Where are you? Come, come. Darling! Hey! But what *are* you doing? Stop! Take that! (a slap). Bad beast! Get out! Filthy! Weeell, take this (food). Do suck something a little healthier. Would you like some fruit? Look at this nice fruit! Leave that. Come on, be a good boy.'

Alone in her bed my Duchess woke refreshed, dressed, splashed her face – I preferred the change without water, but well, the gurgle from the jug, the water and the mirror, her raising her wet face in the glass for her goddaughter to interpose a towel, was interesting enough, stretched neck and tightening skin – and, having sent only for him, set to a summer session of fruit and an infusion.

He could blearily have portrayed her biting at a crisp slice of watermelon or bursting a grape against the roof of her mouth. Or tasting her herbal tea – a ghastly hot smell – that brought sweat to her forehead checked by a chilled and perfumed cloth. Too many sharp scents. I withdrew a little. Or her reading – but only briefly, a paragraph or two of an English novel translated into French. He took longer to be quick.

Humming lightly, she stood up, looked down at her feet, tapped her toes on the floor, took a few mocking dance steps – heel and instep, her arms raised to not quite shoulder height, a little swoop-rush that looked prior to a spin – but then simply stopped, faced him, turned her back on him, and without much art or elegance but with some aplomb, carted up her skirts and grinned round at him.

16

SELENA

AND THIS SUDDEN VIEW — MY DUCHESS BARING
her bum — is what he engraved. There is a lunar, bi-
rondel interest, some striation and by her heels an
open-mouthed capuchin monkey squats and looks
upwards in awe.

Ah, she did not yoke her skirts above her hips and
pose. His airy glimpse did not last more than five beats
of his heart and the etching reflects that. It is nerve – or
perhaps nervous – quick, the lines brisk and crude in
their thickness. It has all the directness of haste. There
is no flattery. In fact, given the usual idealised reducing
of her waist and feet, possibly the reverse. The backs of
those knees are plumpish – is that a blue vein? – the
cheeks have that flattish droop old flesh has, though
she tightened them once, twice, to make them quiver.
A flesh wink? Her hair is untidy, her backward grin
lopsided.

The artist instantly if heavily dropped on one knee, like a man
about to be honoured, then got on to both, at each movement

resoundingly kissing each buttock. At the first, she dropped her skirt over his head.

I retreated a little more, moved round with the result that they were sideways on to me. It was difficult to work out what was happening. The front of her dress was pushed out in the groping way people will look for the division in a curtain, and that was a deal of straddling and delighted bustling from her. And it was then that the deaf artist spoke.

Alas, the noise was muffled – all I could see was his cloth-stretched backside and legs – and I am not sure what he said. It sounded like 'sal' which is salt or alternatively come out; or – I am an *afrancesado* – it could have been 'sale' which is dirty but I am morally sure, and not just because of the title, that he said 'sel' – which is salt again. Selena. The moons of a salt-girl.

His fingers appeared at the forward fringe of her dress and gathered the material. A fraction after, his face – eyes rolling, with a gargoyle's grin though she could not see him – appeared between her legs. Graciously, grinning to her gums, she sat on his back. His briny face glistened. His tongue waggled in triumph.

Discreetly but with some haste I moved back to the table and decided to inspect the fruit; on all fours, however, he swung round after me, bearing the Duchess forward, acting as an animated chair. Chip! is a sound that escapes me when my lids and eyebrows are blinking and twitching. My hand touched something cold and clammy – a damson, a fruit I never eat. I threw off a shudder and retreated some more.

17

THE DUCHESS'S

DRESSING TABLE

———

TOCADOR

DE LA DUQUESA

THIS PORTRAYS A WHITE-FACE MONKEY AND ITS broken reflection; the capuchin has tried to use the looking-glass as a surface for art and, having managed to draw two and a half straggling, longitudinal bars, is judiciously considering his progress while abstractedly seeking more material with his left hand, though the effect is more figleaf than white and jelly tube squeeze.

The artist has lavished considerable care on the flasks and bottles and a powder puff, soft spikes and darkness, the last contrasting with the monkey's here brindled fur and all with the sapajou's clumsy smears. I am not sure the reflection quite matches – that right elbow is too high. The monkey has left some marks on the surface of the mahogany dressing table – shifting feet – and there is a powdery streak on the leading edge. My tail hangs like a thick, hairy plumbline. The mirror is topped by two miniature classical urns.

Did I ever try this? I mean did the artist ever see me? No. I am not fond of my own reflection but I would not try to close it off. Yes, yes, I know. It is not me.

On the other hand, I am not, have never been, like the guacamayo say, an exemplary celibate. I differ from him in that, while we shared being the only representatives of our kind in the shabby *palacete*, I have wrists, palms, fingers. I spill, mostly spilled, my posterity in little, teaspoon puddles. It is also true that I am curious, have decorated plants, anointed – cha! a very pleasant fear – one or two trembling spiders' webs, tested the spread and elasticity of sperm – Lilith glue and thread – can imagine that the mirror on her dressing table might provide a gratifyingly cool surface, but have never thought the jerky stuff was a substitute for gouache, oils or tempera. I have no artistic needs that I can think of. An angle is an angle. Or am I wrong? Compare my member and his brush? Ridiculous. No wood. No sable tip.

The artist frowned. I move my head very quickly. I have also picked up the habit, when somebody stares at me, of jerking my chin at them – 'eh?' He smiled, I took a white flake from my wrist. It was not salt, might have been skin.

In any case I usually choose private corners. But by no means always. One languid afternoon, sat on my favourite spot of the stone-bordered tank, I regaled the fish with three or perhaps four slurries that rattled the water – tails beat, mouths opened and turned – and in various globular shapes – pearls, saddle-bags – sank to the silt at the bottom of the tank. I grew dozy. My lids drooped. My heart slowed. And as often happens with approaching sleep I found that my member had swollen and stiffened. As I dozed off I found it pleasant to toy with the very tip. The stone was warm, the palms barely rustled – and my soft, damp, unsheathed glans was struck, sharp and cross-wise, by something cruel and bony.

The pain was so fierce it waited. I opened my eyes on an indignant, hissing maid. Pain made me deaf. Nausea squeezed me. My hip joints felt bruised to the marrow. I could hardly drag my back legs. The woman – her pulpous lips still distorting her face – gave a complacent, pertussal laugh when I dropped to the ground. The Egyptian cat rose – not to strike at her with his claws – but to pad to its dish to lap water. I crab-retreated across the courtyard, dragged myself upwards.

It's true that once at roof level I tried a feint at throttling a pigeon – but that was a painful fancy, in passing – and I quickly hid on the reverse slope to croon and worry over my parts. My testicles looked like purple kidney beans. The glans was ruptured: a bubble of spongy-looking stuff about the size of a lentil had sprouted on the right-hand side. Through the pain I understood that the maid had hit me with a loose-fingered sideways chop of her hand. And after blowing on my knuckles like a dice player, I sifted through her hissing sounds and made out that she said 'Fuera bicho' – Get out you beast – and felt a tremor in my veins and a heat that made me sweat and bend backwards to offer my stricken genitals to the sky.

How painful it was to urinate. It had to be done in breaths – a hoohoohoo until my lungs ran out of air, then a pause, oh, a long tooth-piercing intake and another exhalation, another quivering little arc. I had for some time to walk carefully, using my knuckles and arms as crutches, keeping out of the way, usually high, usually in shade, a hunched and furry capuchin waiting for night.

The maid was almost as short as a dwarf, had almost more head than lower leg and an equally short, stocky lover who crept into the dark kitchen courtyard (when the pack were chained and excluded) and who confined himself or was confined to gripping, squeezing and fondling her through layers of cloth.

From the roof, by moonlight, it is possible to see a great deal on the ground. The two persons look about them – but not above them – and she, with the one-sided delicacy of a coy hypocrite, presents her thighs and backside to the ardent male, allowing him to feel her flap breasts and barrel chest through material, but keeping her legs tightly pressed to the knee in a parody of virginal enjoyment directed almost exclusively and nibblingly at his neck and ear. He does not try to lift her skirts. His hand slides lower. She removes it. This sterile business is repeated. There is no coupling. Tupping does not exist. Cloth abounds. She considers herself to be facing the right way.

I came down and cocked my head. From my shadowed vantage point I heard her nohnoh, watched her remove his hand and he try to take her other behind her: she pulled it away with a cry of indifferently-done ecstasy. He blinked and pumped harder. As soon as his shadowed hand snug-mimicked pubic hair again, her legs tight as ever, his hips urging somewhere around her left buttock, I dropped to the ground and tooth-chattered – a sound I can make very like a remonstrative snigger.

He was deaf to anything but she heard all right. Stiffening, interrupting herself only with a perfunctory moan, she glanced quickly about the courtyard – but too high.

I stayed still and waited. He kept on, she decided she must have been mistaken and set about resettling her lids and lips, getting back to her damp pleasures.

18

THE MONKEY'S

REVENGE

———

VENGANZA

DEL MONO

AND IT WAS JUST ABOUT HERE THAT THE ARTIST made and fixed his selection – looking down from the roof. He has moved me a little forward into a moonlit spot, my head slightly turned away, leaning on my knuckles, with a suggestion of a threatening shoulder roll. He has rather adapted the maid, made her more swooning than she really was; that raised arm has no sinew or energy in it, is a plump, white falling back to the forehead, not a vigorous warding off. The lover is obscure, a foreshortened head and whiskers, feeding on his loved one's impossibly smooth neck and shoulder, her chin a reduced triangle of tiny dots. Moon motes, not fat underchin and sweat. He has pooled her belly, her knees are buckling, he has given a sheen to her dress.

Shrieking, I tore forward, a crab-rush of five yards, pulled up and, rolling my head, baring my teeth, pointed loinwards.

Her hips jerked forward at once, her hand flew to her hair, her lips started working. She took, she tried to take, a stride towards me, her shaking fingers curved, her teeth grinding – but her left half was imprisoned by her lover. Her leg puppeted out and back.

I snarled. I bounced on my hands. I fixed my eyes on her swain's midnight bulge. I rushed in, feinted towards her ankles – she screamed – then feinted a clawed snatch at his virility. It was enough. She struck but bungled her desire to protect him and thrash me.

I could not have asked for better. She hit him with the heel of her hand at the upturned junction with his testicles. A grunt, he doubled, staggered – some surprised pleasure, mostly pain. And while his britches jumped, his face came up, his eyes widened. Her face already girning, she thoroughly wiped her hitting hand on her skirts before beginning her sobs.

I was not quite finished. I skipped noisily up to the first floor and began with slow aplomb, all moonlight and shadow on the balustrade, to make plummy masturbatory gestures over her shame and dishevelment.

The whiskered young man, puzzled, pained, still savouring the last throbs of gratification through the dreadful ache, pointed, essayed a laugh and while distractedly trying to find something in his pocket also tried to catch her in a forgiving, rueful arm. She struck him smack, mostly on the chin, looked beefily shocked herself, burst now into proper wet tears that gleamed on her cheeks, while he, blinking and rocking from shoe to shoe, a kind of dusty dodder, muttered and nursed his anger and tried to dignify his frown.

To be honest, my blood was not in it. I desisted, let the shadows go and wandered off over the roof tiles meditating on my usual subjects – fires, stars, water and reflections.

I came down by way of a palm tree in the raft courtyard (though the dripping bamboo had been carted off days before) and I made the small jump to check on the water tank. But it was not a propitious night for stars – only one in brackish-looking water in a corner. The Egyptian cat lapped and left. The tortoise had been oiled. I went to sit on the balustrade of the upper cloister.

I was thinking – remembering a winter moon hanging over the sea, reduced to a crescent in its lower half that appeared to be cradling a star, something that excited me so much that I turned cartwheels, ran up and down the cloister, only to find when I returned that the pairing had gone, that the star had vanished and the moon had grown – when I was interrupted by bare feet on the flagstones. I turned my white face and the artist saw me. He stopped, half-closed his eyes on me, cleared his throat. A dialogue?

I waited. While my eyes cannot wink they can be extraordinarily unexpressive. With one foot I scratched the other. Then an itch on my chest with a hand. Then I slicked down the fur between my ears.

He nodded and scratched fairly near his armpit. I blinked. A brief show of his teeth. Bending his knees, putting his hands on them, he tilted forward like a deliberate old man. I don't think he was ever going to offer his hand – so I offered mine, knuckles up, raised the other to my mouth as simpering girls will. Not so much a nod from him as pulse and confirmation.

Behind him crept my Duchess with her finger to her lips. I gave her away without a thought.

'Sapajudas. *Ven, ven.*'

I was not, at this last, quite sure who she was addressing. That is, was she separating us or contradicting herself? The same finger as with her lips was placed under her right eye. She shook her head.

What did she mean? I looked at him for reference. Briefly, rather stiffly, he mimed surprise of the 'really?' sort. Smiling, she held up her hand and ran off. He looked round at me again; a mild expectation in him. Expressionless, I used my tail to play peep-bo over my shoulders.

My Duchess, however, soon brought along a thin collar which she fastened round my neck. There was attached to it a small bell about the size of a hazelnut – four, curved silver petals containing something small, hard and very light; the slightest movement did not produce tintinnabulation so much as an idiot rattle randomly broken by an ear-shrieking sharpness of note that made me shudder and the pea trot. My Duchess laughed and dusted her hands in 'there now' fashion.

The collar was uncomfortable, the noise under my chin potentially maddening. What I could not understand was why she had done it. Was it really a joke? The artist raised his chin and considered me aslant.

The chattering of my teeth had become grinding; I reached behind me, found a suitable bit of vine, tugged it free, trimmed it and split it and, like an old man with a collar stud, jammed the twig into the bell and fixed the pea.

I could not, however, free myself of the collar. To illustrate this for them I plucked at it. Then seizing the loose overtongue, I lifted it, made throttling noises, grimaced, stretched my neck. For too long. I found she had taken his hand and that they were running away.

68

Why?

With no great haste I went up and over the roof and was at the bars of the window to her bedroom before she had turned the key on the inside. I did not squeeze through the bars but waited a while before making myself comfortable on the sill.

I did not look much into the room beyond seeing that our artist lay half on the bed and that my Duchess had knelt between his bare legs; he was always a great deal more artistically discreet about his genitals than mine. Instead I listened – breath and thick mummings – and watched a trail of ants to the remains of a cockroach. Black ants in the moonlight. Grape-coloured traffic. I picked up a stray one and, closing my eyes, placed it on the tip of my tongue. The taste was a burst of slightly acidic nothing and against my lids I could see something like a reniform contour map – lines of red and green and a burst of deep blue.

19

A MONKEY'S ANT

HORMIGA DE UN MONO

IS NOT QUITE THAT. THE BARS ARE ON THE WRONG side, i.e. I have not gone through them. They are short and thick and not like the twisted pokers they really are. In addition my posture is one of a lout, one leg hanging down. There is no vinestuck hazelnut bell round my neck. In my right hand I am, I presume, holding up an ant. The other hand helps sustain a thing like a diamond-dealer's glass to the right eye. There is no sign of the ant. My expression is that of a self-satisfied pimp or customs man. Though surely my curiosity as to the taste of an ant is not intrinsically inferior to his as to the feel of being tasted. Why scratch me then?

And now – ah! – we come to one of the loveliest of the etchings.

20

LA BANDERILLERA

MY DUCHESS IS IN THE ROLE OF *BANDERILLERO* — the person in a bullfight whose task it is to plant two decorated goads in the brave hump of muscle riding above the bull's shoulders.

But here there is no bull. Here is no pot-bellied trot and fluster, here no dewlap hanging from neck to forelimbs. And the naked model did not use real *banderillas* – spikes that *look* flower-decked but surely cannot be. Petals with horses and lances and blood? Or are they paper trimmings of the kind chefs use, stained in flower colours? The *banderillas* he has given her are thinner and shorter than those I ever saw, and I note too that they are like small harpoons, have their points barbed. What she really had in her hands – and you should hear the rusted grind of venerable shears – was one rolled ribbon halved to make two twists. This ribbon he used in the engraving to tie back her hair.

Idealised? Ecstatic! She is on her toes, her right foot in front of the other, on the brink of resolution and success – you can almost feel the chill of those sharpened steel points – her raised arms and neck making for an exhilarating line, her thighs stretched,

71

her long trunk twisting into a triple curve, her eyebrows up, her lips tucked in. She is beautifully concentrated.

Her pose has already trimmed and tightened her but our artist has, I think, trimmed her neck and hunkers more, tightened that softish bust and given her dab pubic curls, to make a direct, delicate, naveled and nippled maiden.

And me? I serve as counterpoint or at least juxtaposition, am portrayed in the corner as little more than a hairy vessel, a small-headed vase with a fringe at my neck and, a little thicker, for my feet and hands on the floor. My tail? Gone. I look as rudimentary as a nostrilled seaslug except for two smaller dots, my eyes, fixed on her knees.

It is a most *economical* etching – the *banderillas* are the same twitch and petal as the arrowhead body hair – and is all line, no shadow, no shading (even on me) though the line is frequently thin, frequently trembles. His grace, his musing. Compare the point of her left breast with that of the *banderillas*. Compare my eyes and the tip of her right.

In life she was delighted by the effects of plunging her hands down; the ribbons rose, doubled and slithered in candlelight. Pointed forward they flow back. Held up, they twist against her arms. Stabbed again, they rise above her hands. Imagination

72

rifled his face. What had he in mind? Grasp, shift, fix, eyes like a huntsman. She plunged those *banderillas* into far more than six bulls at three pairs apiece – with a ha! ya! if pleased – letting them drop to the floor, turning her back on them. There were variations. She mimed wrestling the bull, winding the ribbons round its horns, using them as reins. She once curtseyed very formally when picking them off the floor, was briefly Diana with a ribbon bow and ribbon arrow, crossing them and finding them droop, walked away, prepared again, shaking the ringlets, letting them spin, calling the bull. She did wear her hair up but she was not so elongated, not in the waist nor in that very elegant neck. Nor was her smile quite so fine and lip-tucked. But her amused, exacting eyes he has just so.

My memory of the etching is more powerful than my memory of the circumstances. I have had to make some effort to recall that her dance took place at night, not in limpid daylight – and recall again. And I cannot remember if the goddaughter was about, moping in a corner, covering herself with a white sheet. Or was that another time? And why such difficulty? Was it the repetition of her movements? Or was I abashed? If this, it was because of her confidence, then his. I blinked, I lowered my eyes. I was not in the corner of the room but at the corner of her bed. I retired upwards to the tester and there, to the low squeal of her feet and the sometimes thud of her heel, found and examined a bleached-looking moth corpse. How pale and brittle it looked.

This etching also danced a little – preceded *The Dune Bath*, preceded the last three – but without any dithering. Others he picked up with care, gently lifting with his fingertips at the edges, but this plate he seized and lifted high. Odd gesture; he shut his eyes tight and slowly turned his face up and round like someone savouring the warmth of the sun.

A while later I abandoned the moth and peeked over. The limp lengths of ribbon had been cast aside on the floor. I was not going to claim them. Instead I obtained a remarkable view of my Duchess's face – all eager grimace and licks – as our artist vigorously attended her.

21

SAINT GEORGE

SHOWS A WHITE-FACE MONKEY, SITTING ON THE ground near the base of a palm tree. The monkey is facing the viewer's right and above his head there is, in splendid unconcerned flight towards the other edge, a dragonfly. An early one, let it be said, if there is any correlation between the forty-two engravings and the forty-two days he spent in Sanlúcar. Always welcome of course, but the upward crawl out of water of millions of nymphs and their transformation into glistening dragonflies in the air occurs almost a lunar month after the tenth of August and, by September, the artist was not there.

The monkey's expression is just between basking and the realisation of what has flown over his head. How is the switch of his attention from sun towards wings worked? The lowered lids are a mite up, the unfocused eyes about to take in more light, the nostrils ready to expand, the lips gathering to tighten, the neck already moving. The stimulus has been the whirr, or possibly the fleeting shadow. The monkey is still a fraction away from perceiving what has passed him.

I do not know if this is important or not but the title is a poor English joke on dragons and damsels – a sight less funny than fly. I wear no armour. No nostrils smoke. No flight is fiery. Or have I missed the point, the brilliant and, at those dates, non-existent whirr? Because this etching was hindsight, was one of the very last to be done and many other plates had to shove along to accommodate it. That would explain the time factor. He made little fuss of it but it is one of *my* favourite etchings; it draws the eye, there is a lovely airiness to it.

22

CUADROS

DE UN ZÍNGARO

FROM ENGLISH TO SPANISH. OUTINGS. HE RARELY
went – except with her for purposes unsocial – and
never after dusk. She was a sociable person, almost
never alone.

Though, surely, this one is fancy; a memory of hers
impressed by him. She liked to be gullible, loved
fortune tellers, acrobats and dancers. Note the word
zíngaro rather than *gitano* for gypsy and that *cuadros*
are pictures and sets.

Time: day. The most populated of the etchings – the
handsome young guitarist, the reclining, bald old
man, two spectacular, meaty sluts, the bawd, an old
female dwarf – and facing them, their caravan-cart
and rocky hills nowhere near here, my Duchess and
her dog, a horizontal whirlwind stymied by a large
bow on the right rear leg; that trembling paw is barely
on the ground.

Compare for a moment the women. The travellers
wear not gypsy clothes but mantillas like towers of
black icing, have chins to chuck and round shoulders

to knead. My Duchess has enormous moth wings on her head – a rakish tilt, a stylised wing twisting of Giant Peacock (male) on Giant Peacock (female). Look at that eye pattern. Her body is erect, one of her shoes half-raised, the heel off the ground and her attention is rather more on her profile than on the *cuadros*. Who is the guitarist about to serenade, head down, thumb cocked?

For my part I have, as it were, gone over to the *zíngaros* – am in the right quadrant, beyond the old fellow's belly, have acquired a baboonish acquaintance by a wagonwheel; we look like a pair of farmers about to agree terms on a milk cow, both convinced of our individual astuteness. Are we both male? It is difficult to see.

The etching is delicately divided by a fire, though smoke is hardly shown, lapdog and owner to the left, *zíngaros* in the rest.

My Duchess, bored by dinner out, returned early to catch him at this one as he sat, happy and deaf and almost alone. This time I obeyed her finger to her lips. She was always interesting to watch. Having run up, ready to get sympathy, her eyes widened, she began to grin. I could not quite see who or what she pointed at – the pot-bellied old man, the sluts, I read more in her expression – before she punched his arm, bent to kiss him, trace his eyebrows, tug-milk his earlobes . . . and I moved away.

When I glanced back to find her sitting on his knees and leading his right hand upwards, I left, went up to roof level. The surrounding land is flat, dry shrubland. Low stars. New moon. Human coughing somewhere. I practised sitting quite still in the clammy night, waiting for the drone of a mosquito. A while after, dozing on his window ledge, I woke at what looked for a moment to be a fat firefly – my hand moved to catch it; but it was my Duchess waving a lighted taper, as if signalling to a great distance. Behind the glass, at times looking trapped in the glass, moved glowing curlicues, small flame and long tail, the main shape an eight on its side but with trembling variations and twirls. I did not stir except to touch the glass and find it still cold. Behind the tracery, behind my playful Duchess, he grunt-snored and turned over in the campaign bed. She smiled and blew out the taper; smoke and stretched lips. I do not think the smile was for me. For his reflection possibly. But somehow I understood it was entirely for herself.

23

THE BATH

———

EL BAÑO

HAS ONE OF THOSE MISTAKES THAT SOME MINDS like, the kind that read philosophy books for misprints, but arithmetically, with no thought of coincidence or surprise; the goddaughter has her features all right but he has forgotten her skin colour and made her an albino.

There is a theatrical mirror on a curtained wall as backdrop. I am seated to the right on the floor holding a scallop shell in one hand as people will a breviary or, sometimes, a fob-watch. My eyes are resolutely fixed on this. What am I after? The goddaughter, on her feet to the left, is craning her neck to look at me.

My Duchess sits on a cushioned box, aslant and astride, and gives mostly her back to the viewer; she is dreamily bringing a sponge – note the effect of her water-displacing fingers, that is a firm hold – up her left thigh. The sponge is in her right hand but the left arm – think about it, it could have gone backwards to provide support – has been lifted, almost in a warding-off gesture at the mirror, to provide a pretty play of profiled breast and line. That tilted mirror shows the invisible right leg and the sponge shoulder. On the floor there is a basin – like an inverted hat – of clay.

I don't know. I find the whole design too laboriously set up. Do those angles really match? That posture of hers would surely cause pain in the small of her shapely back. I could mention pubic discretion again. I have the impression of something missing too, like the pin of a sundial. But those lines on the shell are merely lines.

No, it is too classical, too impersonal. My Duchess was a delightful bather – sometimes delightfully quick – and there would seem to me to be other more particular, more revealing views. From her wrapping (or unwrapping) herself in a hot wet sheet which had first been smoked over pans containing olive-stone coals and eucalyptus leaves, sometimes with a touch of lemon, to her standing naked in a china bowl to receive scoops of chill water; from her sud-filled bath that baize-closed to allow meals or letter-writing to the almond milk that made her gleam rub by rub, stretch by joint, shoulder to breast, hip to knee; from the hasty dab and slop of her half-wash of oxters and privates, a mildly gamy flavour joined by her lengthened throat to cool water on her temples, the waggle of her wiped breasts on her way between dresses, with her goddaughter at her hair and a maid with at least three towels for her moppings and scatterings of powder, her feet leaving tracks, and colour going into her cheeks and another maid at the back buttons and the variety of brushes –

for her lashes, for her lips, for her nails – and her very cool grimacing into a mirror and her earrings and, already time to dine, the straightening of material and, still very matter of fact, sucking her teeth and lips, the grinding of various glass stoppers – a pause, some murmurs – before the drops were shaken out. A thick, warm musky explosion of scents. My Duchess was the only woman I have smelt who wore two or more perfumes at the same time.

24

THE STOCKING

LA MEDIA

WAS DONE WITH THE CARE HE EXPENDED ON stroking her inner thigh with his inner thumb. Note particularly the extraordinary range of detail and fingerprint, clear line, close texture.

My Duchess is shown in evening dress, one leg on the floor, the other raised, her shoe on a foot stool. Her dress is pulled back and she bends to attend to the stocking top. All flour and dough and muslin. Is she rolling off or rolling on the stocking? Has she come back? Or is she about to go out? The latter, the latter.

She looks amused that he should find silk and leg noteworthy. Her thigh is as much robust as well-turned for such a modest little person – not tall by any means, narrow-shouldered, thin-fingered, thin-waisted, but amply supported. And that is not simply because her leg and stocking are fully-drawn while her back is a bare line. What stands out? The leg, her face – eyes, nose, mouth – and best of all, her right hand.

I have almost disappeared, save for a foot, my ears,

a hairy hand, belong, as it were, to a low cloud at bottom left – through which can be glimpsed a nostril slit, a smirk, a dribble of saliva.

What am I there for? The composition? Perhaps to be redundant. But let me return to the subject which, in spite of the singular title, is a conjunction; her hand in relation to her stocking. This is correspondence and I am unclear as to how he suggests the weave of the silk without minute crisscrossing, something he has kept for the skin on her fingers, particularly the valleys between her knuckles. With what delicacy he suggests the arabesques in her touch.

Neither the previous etching nor this one bears relation to circumstances I remember. That bath was academic. But I do remember a more intimate view of stockings and flesh; my Duchess invisible but for her naked thighs and still-stockinged legs hooked round his hips and her hands plying his back. Strange humours. For a variety of reasons – a locked door, a fixed mosquito net on the window – I could not get out. I retired under a draped table and tried not to listen to all those sounds, bed, skin, breath, slithering silk – and his bellow.

25

THE MARAUDER

EL MERODISTA

Our four-sided courtyard pool – first seen occupied by a raft – was the centre of a six-part pattern of drinking places, sunning areas and so on. With its water the tortoise was occasionally doused – evidently enjoyable in an old-maid sort of way – and the peacock's colours freshened. It was not exceptional to see, at one time, reflections of the droop-tailed blue fowl as it used one length for a forgetful-looking stroll, myself at one corner *ensimismado*, the goat's head at another as it rested its chin on stone and, in the centre of the other length, the Egyptian cat. Its tail would twitch – though whether following the beat of fish gill or fish tail or neither I am not sure – as it stared into the water; when it had followed enough it would settle and doze over its charges. What were its motives? It looked more jealous than possessive and had a remarkable ability to sort out the sounds of the pool, ignoring a fallen leaf or the swirl as a fish took in an insect but showing immediate interest if one of those round mouths merely broke the surface.

In the hot months when oxygen became short in the water the fish rose very near the surface to hang there almost without movement. The cat watched over them and one dawn gave a

marauding duck a tremendous bloodfeather squawk of a death –
striking as it beat wings to rise from the water, a fish in its beak,
sending it crashing towards the cloisters and pursuing the
barrelling, feather-spraying creature and catching it with a noise
like a wood chopper against a door. The dropped fish flapped in
the courtyard dust, its mouth urgently seeking water, the goat
bleated, but the cat returned to its place and blink-slept, reassured
by the now calm surface of the water and the cluster of fish
suspended just beneath it.

OUR ARTIST WAS NOT THERE BUT FROM THE TWO
corpses, one mangled and broken-necked, one impres-
sively dull after its previous gleam, reconstructed the
following from a position similar to that for my
Duchess's raft, same cloister but an arch or two
towards the centre: the duck has just snatched the fish,
its webbed feet are trailing in the water and it is at the
point of maximum muscle effort in its attempt to rise
from scummy liquid into air.

There are various creatures and reactions. To the
right, the tail-spread peacock, all serene, stately
shimmer. He was overfond of that display – and of
ignoring the peahen. The goat has retreated into its
defensive, head-down position. And there, even the
tortoise has turned its head at the intrusion. Has it
dropped a withered dandelion?

I, to the left, have my eyes on the artist; he has
widened my mouth, made it a hairline crack. I look

wizened and fatuously pleased as if the stone-tank were some kind of trap and the fish bait. Though a viewer who did not know of the subsequent deaths would think what? And what pleasure exactly am I offering?

The cat, however, is masterly in execution. It has raised its head – the neck is rather long – but it has made no other movement. Good, it was deceptive, almost always looked slow even a fraction before striking. The body is sphynx-like, the anticipation in the dreamy squint of those mildly enlarged eyes.

Incidentally, had the cat been in the position he has given it – on the left, further down from me on the peacock walk – the duck would probably have been sent back into the water or not hit at all. The cat made for the far end at a furry trot and struck across and down.

26

THE DUNE CART

———

CARRITO Y DUNAS

THIS ETCHING, ALL GRAIN AND DUSK, SHOULD have come after the next, belongs to the same day but took place two hours later. Still, here you are. Of course, error is always possible – his final ordering was, if not quite hasty, certainly vigorous, sometimes distracted – and he may, having misnumbered and titled, simply cursed and gone on. But this does not detract from a pleasant little scene.

Along a gently crescented shore my Duchess drags me behind her in a doll-sized cart. We are very small figures – you have to peer. It is almost all landscape; dunes, very wet beach (the tide is just out of sight) and the figure of a woman with adjunct. Can you actually see the rope? My tail? My features?

The sand was so wet it enclosed her bare feet, released them, so that impression, depression, was no rounder than her ankles:

digitless dibbing appeared behind me between the tracks of those dragging, clogging wood wheels.

The sun sank towards the sea. The small dog ran. Our artist led the slow ass. Behind us all, the goddaughter trailed. From time to time, the godmother stopped and handed me a shell or a smooth stone to examine. After the first – a cowrie – she let me decide whether or not the item joined me in the cart. I am particularly fond of what are locally called 'ears' – small, amber and gleam convolutions no more three-dimensional than a button, a little chillier to touch than ground glass, not so chill as stone. But it had not been a good tide for them. Two and a broken one were hardly worth it. I tossed them out in our wake.

The cart stopped. The plodding ass snorted. Called by its mistress the small dog raced towards her. Was there any breeze? Ripple-induced perhaps. The lapdog leapt but it was a stunted effort as if into a wind. In any case it was the ribbon my Duchess wanted. Having removed it (the tuft-dog pushed away) she looked round at the artist with such tenderness that my eyes smarted. A sudden access of love? How deep? How advisable? My Duchess began to tie the dog's ribbon on her own hair and if the next part is blurred, full of blinks and squints, remember that I preferred to keep my feet as dry as I could in the doll's cart, that she moved away fiddling with that stringy little piece of red and that the light had some duskish correspondence to the huzz and echo of poppling foam.

The ribbon on her nape was still not enough. She wanted to offer him more. How far did she pull up her dress? Gooseflesh and thighs, navel and black hair. *Did* she try to carry him on her back? At the least she pushed her hips into his and draped his arms over her shoulders. But was that her staggering? She certainly stroked his exultant face, her thumb catching at his pride-swollen lips, her fingers trembling. Huzz-husky, she caught and kissed his hand. And then? Reader, they ran to the retreating sea, watched by a puzzled small dog, its tongue lolling, and a brine-surfeited capuchin. The ass appeared to be sleeping where it stood, the stumbling, shawl-yoked goddaughter finally flopped on the sand, to have a headache. My Duchess kicked at foam. There are grating sounds that can reach the roots of teeth. The pitch here was much lower but somehow the sound of her laughter mingled with that of the surf and made my shoulderblades ache like those roots.

But to return. It is a moving etching, though I am not sure why. The scale of her? The dusk? I preferred her at night, on her return from dinner, smelling of wine, occasionally tobacco, her perfumes tired, the sleepy jounce of all that head of hair, her shrugging off her shoes, her yawn, her putting her feet in a foot bath. Sedater stuff? No, I preferred her indoors in candlelight; night favoured her, suited her features and skin, smoothed her off, held her in.

27

THE HORSE STABLES

LAS CUADRAS

WHICH, I REPEAT, PRECEDED THE EVENTS OF THE previous engraving, have a splendid solidungular appeal. The ass, all teeth and futtering grey lip, is in the foreground stall. I, on the nearest wood divide, have turned my head towards the ass and wear an expression of supercilious enquiry. How old we look. We are not scratched so much as thread-veined everywhere except at the chops.

The rest is an effortless *tour de force* involving perspective, shadow and cobbles along an aisle of horse stalls for a thousand mounts – or rather half a thousand. There were no horses and this abandonment (ancestral *peste equina*) is faithfully reflected. The only window shown is the roundheaded one on the very far wall – it could fit into one of the quadruped's rectangular teeth.

It was a gloomy place of straw-stale air. In stall 43 named for *Brillante*, an Arab gelding, my Duchess and her artist threshed. Her breath shrieks. Wood thuds and groans. In an old sack straws rub, sometimes shrilly: a rhythm of moted air. Her shoeheel stutters and then catches a clogged groove of dung and earth grouting, catches cobble, and retraces it, retraces it. The female ass exhales. Its flank twitches. Four hoofs stir.

But then the flank twitched again and I woke up to the previous drone. On an area as big as a man's hand the skin crinkled, was elastically released. A willing shudder is not much of a defence. The fly simply rose and landed again on a fresh patch of hide.

Gimcrack grandeur. The fly irritated, put me on my mettle. I leapt and caught it – snap your fingers – by the wings, took the bright, repulsive insect round to the donkey's face to show. Inner lid, reflection in the cloudy mottled jelly, hem and lens. The creature shifts back, its head comes up.

I turned and quietly removed the fly's wings and tossed what remained into the next stall. The place is silent, stifling. A rustle, a soft laugh, a soft squeak of straw. I looked round. The open door represents not the notion of light but that of possible breeze. But the air is too close. I cannot tell. Outside, pre-empting the lapdog's whine, the slow, excluded voice of the goddaughter calls without any sign of hope – '¡*Señora*! ¡*Mamaita*!'

But they must have finished their bout around the time I divested the fly of its wings. Yes, some more stuff to do with scarecrows and running and a few shouts but I cleaned my hands, picked a little salt, got ready to move.

28

THE UMBRELLA

EL PARAGUAS

SURELY HE MEANT PARASOL, RAYS NOT DROPS?
My simply-dressed Duchess, shoes in one hand, strolls across the etching behind a gently-rising line of soft, hot sand, against a sky of clear midday blue and protected from the sun's glare by a fringed umbrella, fit for an African chief, held over her by a burly, bushy-haired artist in waistcoat, rolled sleeves and bare calves. Her chin is autocratic but her smile an animated mix of the biddable and the impudent.

Behind them, on a tasselled cushion, borne by a turbanned goddaughter, is the lapdog. The turban has a spray – a trimmed peacock feather – held by a disc or a round jewel. The little dog has no ribbons and seems skinnier and bigger-eyed than usual.

They are approaching – on this side of the sand line at the right – a sapajou artist complete with palette and easel and brushes and another hat, a curious contraption, like a flopping icebag, and a canvas, which the viewer but not the processionists can see. It portrays the Duchess, umbrella bearer and the dog bearer at right angles to the larger show. Here there is no sign of dressing-table knickknacks. Maybe due to the baggy hat – to give the flop more length – there is something elongated about my snout as I squint at them and measure them up against the vertical. I have also had difficulty placing my tail. Sitting on it? Or did he forget? At any rate it is not gripping brush or paint tube.

There is also the detail – on the canvas image – that, instead of giving her clusters of black curls, the sapajou has made wings of his Duchess's hair, but as when the butterfly has crawled from its chrysalis and is still furled and wet. His haste and pulse? Accident? The work is certainly in progress and it may be the capuchin has merely indicated her hair for the moment. These are both perhapses. Her image on the canvas is no bigger than her real index fingernail.

Accompanying us – the goddaughter did not wear a turban nor did she carry the dog on her cushion and on this outing we went inland, away from the sand and sea – was the ass, on whose back between a pair of wicker baskets the small dog initially rode. Not for long. Quickly alarmed at the movement it was, with a little yelp, brave enough to jump before anyone brought the donkey to a halt, but then snagged and mewled at my Duchess's heels. She picked it up. The shoes she gave to me and I took them with me to the donkey's back; her footwear riding on the saddle, her feet bare to the ground.

In retrospect, I was anxious for the she-ass. I patted its neck, made clucking noises and, hanging from a basket, clambered round to look into the creature's huge eye. But I am no longer sure why. Was I frightened it would stumble? Or was it showing signs of discomfort? At that rocking umbrella ahead? Or at the starting click and subsequent whirr of the many looping insects that accompanied us through the scrub? The landscape was vast and flat. The few bushes were not tall enough to provide shade and the clumps amongst the trails were suited only to locusts, lizards and scorpions. Perhaps it was that – the scrubby height – that disturbed the donkey into a stolid, oat-sweet sweat and a most unusual twitching of eye and leg. The earth gave back excessive sun. The wicker creaked. The plants gave off no freshness. My skin – under my fur – grew hot. The carried dog's tongue hung. The goddaughter gleamed. Our artist's back, not under the umbrella, sweat in lungish patches. And I dropped one of her shoes. They were of some kind of white chamois, with a small heel and a silk bow. Clutching the other I dropped down and retrieved it. It lay beside dessicated rabbit droppings and a partridge feather. High above three hawks looked down. With a shudder I scooted back and a short time later there was a flash ahead, like light on tin, and my Duchess cheered.

Under the planted umbrella – not easy for the strenuously patient artist who finally gave up on piercing the topsoil and instead built a cairn of stones to secure the shaft – we set out and set to. From the baskets tumbled a picnic; cold meats, pies, fruit, wine and – in a *cantimplora*, a clay receptacle handled and knob-spouted and drunk from direct like a goatskin, on an arc – miraculously cold water.

I disliked the pastry – moist but sticky – and the rank, gelatined game, but there were some tiny roast birds of which I ate one leg and two crunchy wings, ripped off for me by my Duchess, and followed them with a slice of water-pear.

The artist stayed with me in the shade of the hot canvas when the women and the small dog went off to explore. As was usual with him he began fiddling his fingernail in the soil. Some shapes. I had just eaten. An arc cut by something else. My lids were heavy. His preferred beach? The huzz of a non-existent sea?

29

YOU'VE SERVANTS

CRIADOS TIENES

A WIND HAS BLOWN UP ON THE SEASHORE AND OF the three human figures the male, black-suited, clutching his black hat, is walking away. The two women look out to where a small simian figure in and on a tiny model sloop is riding wind-stirred water. That is all. The wind is strong enough to raise the women's dresses nearly to the knee; indistinctly featured, formally dressed, from their heads stream black mantillas. I am difficult to make out; white face, rakish prow, the mast tip between my nipples. It is – all that dust, those funereal clothes – a most extraordinarily glum etching.

I do not understand it well. That he should choose shore and *levante* when everything was inland and as still as a bakery. That he should separate out umbrella and servants in this way. For the goddaughter carried on her cushion not a lapdog (as he has it in

28), but a sailing boat – and no elegant model but a crude canoe with a tarpaper sail on its single stick-mast. It was merely an elongated coconut, halved lengthways, with a crease more decorative than useful where the keel might be. The hull, that is, was pale green. The inside had been gouged out by some simple-handed soul. The only aid to stability was a fixed, rusted rudder, the blade of a machete that had parted from the heft as it chopped into the coconut. Add sail and a hastily whittled mast and I suppose it bore a fortuitous resemblance to something seaworthy enough to nose about the courtyard tank. But that was a prop, not a boat, a notion, not a vessel.

I was used to her celebrations and I knew his imagination was alarmingly oiled; away from the sea, in scrubland, still some way from the ponds and reeds and marshes proper, I dozed.

They say prickly but the heat is a mix of tight skin and soft graze. I was briefly and dreamily aware of a shadow – non-canvas – over me before I was snatched up. Tucking me under her arm, my Duchess gave a juddering sort of skip, shouted gleefully (to the goddaughter?) and began to run. I struggled, to get upright more than anything, but was rewarded by a sharp shh! I lay limp, a resigned droop of fur, her breast jouncing on my back, the ground lolloping beneath my eyes, to the sound of her breathing as she ran in the heat. Her heart ran faster than mine. How determined she could be to enjoy herself! I shut my eyes and listened to her excitement. I do not say I dozed off again but when she stopped and abruptly hoisted me high in the air like a baby, the lift of my stomach over her head made me shudder. Combined with the sun's glare, it meant I was slow to squint and peer about me.

Even through watering eyes it was – too late – obvious from the goddaughter's crouch over the canoe, the pond and my Duchess's encouraging chucks – still panting – that they had some miniature seamanship in mind.

Amazed, I sneezed. I twisted. I clung with my hands and feet to her neck and head. I do not have to say that I know nothing of boats, or of how to swim and much prefer a static image of me, however grim the context, than to move in real and horrible uncertainties.

Good-humouredly treating me like a deficient octopus – glare and clumps of reeds made it impossible to see the extent of the water beyond the notion of a very sorry expanse – she prised me clear and at arm's length drop-placed me on the boat.

I stopped my mewling and wriggling immediately. The craft's chronically light movement was paralysing. I clutched the mast – it moved – then very hastily crouched and clasped the sides of my coconut.

I am not good at estimating how deep water is, especially when light catches the ripples. I was not pushed so much as released. The buoyancy of the thing! It was too late to jump and there was nothing to jump from except that bobbing half-shell. I shrank. I shut my eyes. To be unnerved by a seething noise; that boat moved through water as if it were pulling off a top layer of skin. When I tried to look round the wretched thing rocked. Absurd slopping and clonking noises started. Drops of water, rainbow-shot, leapt from the pond surface when I tried to stop the wassling. What was I representing? Some simple call, a pleasant note like the tongue of a bell. I could hear laughter, I could see water – but, my back was to them – I could not tell how far from land I was.

Twitching but stiff, I began to think the canoe might be

slowing, that the initial impulse had slackened – but when a boat is made of a coconut almost any water is choppy. Coconut milk, tree sap, a rubberish expression; there was I think more movement up and down than forward. But I began to curve-turn. Carefully, tongue to one side, one eye closed, the other slowly wrenched; some eight or nine yards away my Duchess and her goddaughter were delighted with the picture, clapped hands, jumped and even waved at me. A little paddling and a long pole would have fetched me in – but they wished to share the scene. Together.

Reader, both ran off. I stayed quite still. Very gently, at first almost imperceptibly, my craft drifted, stern first away from the bank. An incurious insect droned by. Was that a breeze? A riffle of wind? Were there currents? Masked by reeds something fowlish clucked. Not five yards away, out of the corner of my eye, I saw something slick-black rise and sink. In all that dismay and heat I felt as if I were deflating, my head small, my eyes shrunk. Water speckled my fur. I was incredulous and miserable, that is I did not bear to think of what was going to happen, only huddled in my misery.

Reeds sighed. Something croaked. I shivered. My nut-canoe nodded. The first water trickled through to my skin. I had drifted a whole stone watertank, was well down another. Something under the water let loose a chain of airbubbles.

Our artist missed all this drift. Pulled along to admire, he nodded at his Duchess's surprise at the change in the scene and refused – very laconically from my lookout – to rescue me. I do not know if he said anything about servants; if he did say something it looked like 'Again? No.' – though I was not up a vine-clad column. He shrugged, mopped his face with a shaken-out handkerchief and, with both hands in pockets, doggie scurrying after, strolled off.

My Duchess – oh, that was an anxiously long stretch of water, out of one courtyard and in amongst the sad oranges of the second – seemed less offended by his refusal than determined to ignore it – though to her determination I should add nerves and distraction.

And the goddaughter? I began to feel sick. *Mal d'étang* or fear? Probably both. She made graphic gestures and grimaces – for my benefit as well? – against wading in amongst swelling leeches, ferocious nymphs, slimy slugs, wriggling tadpoles – and undulating watersnakes. I do not know if you, reader, will ever see your life placed against possible rescuers' disgust at pond life. Had I wrung my hands they would have squeaked. Water slopped into my boat. My Duchess made parrying gestures, as if keeping time – then ran for another third party.

My coconut was becoming waterlogged from the rear forward. A very wet white-face, I had to watch an argument between the two women as to who should ride in on the she-ass. The goddaughter felt that the new arrangement was acceptable to her squeamish feet but that the risk was still too great for my Duchess. My Duchess thought. My Duchess slid off, helped the goddaughter mount. I lost my rudder – a rusty, silent detachment. The she-ass had no desire to enter the water.

My Duchess heaved, the goddaughter dug her heels in the donkey's belly. The ungulate futtered its lips at the water surface – and then decided to cool its hoofs.

More heaves, a ridiculous barefoot kick or two, more water. It became clear to me, and I was sodden, that a problem loomed even if the donkey did move on. But how deep was the water? For a few yards the pond barely rose to those bulbous knees. The donkey sniffed ahead, blinked and cast itself forward.

It did not matter that the shockwave was not large – it swept towards me, with rings of followers. My bark rose, tilted, lost water and began to rock like an idiot toy. I gibbered and clutched.

Coming towards me a stately struggle – the powerful nostrils of the ass, the goddaughter holding on as if to a bolted stallion, her dress hoisted, her legs glistening. My eyelashes were wet, I was squinting through them and rainbow-tinctured drops but I could still make out my Duchess waving instructions at them to go round.

My boat gave its last bubbles, wallowed very slightly, then sank below the surface. But why did it sink no more? I could see my feet as if in some unhappy parody of a bath – the half-nut moving heavily to the impulse from the donkey – and I was half-standing, with one hand touching rather than gripping that stick of a mast, with my tail hoisted, my eye-brows dripping, when I understood that the goddaughter could not hear her godmother. She could never in any case bring the donkey round to a delicate berth and I had a much solider base than previously.

Fear – and images of plucking, sucking liquid, water with lips and mouths – gave me wings. I leapt. At least three and a half metres, twirling tail assisted, to strike the goddaughter on shoulder and head. I mean I did not take into account that she was moving too. She grunted – a dull, shocked sound – and I scrambled down and fitted all four limbs round a breast.

Cheers and clapped hands from the shore – how that woman loved to applaud. Swirling water and snorts in the pond. The coconut boat continued where it was, under the surface, but did not sink. The sail detached, flop-floated.

Raising her skirt in welcome and to form an apron-towel, my Duchess petted and patted me. My ears. My brows. Between my toes and fingers. I shivered and sneezed. She kissed my head and cradled me to her.

'*Ay, mi niño, ay, mi niño.*'

The donkey dripped. The goddaughter wrang out her skirt. Surely I was about to receive many more endearments and soft chafings and sweetmeats and to be taken home? But somehow this did not happen. My Duchess did not stiffen, she *set* (letting me down to the ground halfway through), staring and frowning out across the scrubland. I tugged her dress. She shook her head, then went to squat at the water's edge and indulge in a morose mutter and nod with her own reflection. I gave up, went to sit on the donkey so that my feet would not burn.

30

CE N'EST PAS CUIT

IS MY DUCHESS'S VIEW ACROSS THE DINNER
table as the artist lifts a domed silver cover off a
silver ashette on which there lies a live sapajou
monkey garnished with a small cloth or blanket. His
other arm is raised as an eager cymbalist's but empty,
he is hatted with the same hat as in the previous
engraving and his expression is similar to that in the
sea-urchin supper or his gondolier's bath – a most
wolfish slyness.

Note to one side the chaste, neo-classical holder
with the candle flame tilted to the right (from the
cymbalist's current), the wineglasses, all empty and,
on the other side, a salt cellar, a pepper mill and a glass
decanter shaped like a head of garlic.

His first remark, the uncooked title, *monsieur le sapajou*
understood: *Enchanté, madame. Mais je n'aime pas les jeux très
forts, madame. J'ai peur.*

The artist peeled back the blanket and with one stubby finger raised, brows down, lips out, paused – '*Il y a du sel?*' Is there salt? I also understood, a clear indication I had not been in brine – before beginning on a boisterous deafman's lecture. His expression, his care, his ennumeration of cooking methods – *lapin ici, comment se dit 'lechon' en français?* – rabbit here, how do you say suckling pig in French? – was all grim game to him. The long index knife, the chopping hands, the gentle waves of fingered flames bespoke a stewer. He diced vegetables, shovelled them up and dropped them into my pot. He could make a remarkably accurate imitation of a sizzle. An extra tinkling noise I traced to me – an arc of urine hitting one of his wineglasses, but not much going in.

He was the only one at table who did not giggle or guffaw, but that is not a virtue. And my Duchess? An arrangement of mopped hair and heaving bodice, she shook her head, not quite fast enough for rejection, not quite slowly enough for resignation: choke, cough, *cochon*. But the choke was demure, the cough doucie and the *cochon* much closer to a tertiary hiccup than a downright you pig.

I blinked and cut bladder; our artist, lips down, chin up, turned towards servicial shadows and gravelled something about an omelette.

'*Y si son pequeños, que sean tres.*'

Spanish for three eggs if small.

Another ripple of sycophantic relish. Enough. Like an offended hunchback I rose, should have dragged the blanket off with me, but he leant briskly forward, tweaked it out of my hands and dropped it over the pissed-on glass. I appealed to her at once but my chin-puckered Duchess was musing on her bosom, the pale hairs rising on tightening swells of gooseflesh. My sneeze came like a nasal spit.

But later, as I sat on a console peeling but not eating all the fruit in a bowl, I saw them coming round the cloister together. I chose to dry my fingers on *The Triumph of Summer*, feeling the varnish, getting the dried brush strokes to take on grape and peach juice – but they did not even glance at me when they passed. He seemed gloomily and eructfully replete; she, a cloth obscured hand away from him, slack-skinned and ugly. He had missed a fat grain of sea salt on his upper lip. I turned my hand and rubbed my knuckles on old paint.

31

RISE

SUBIR

NOT QUITE A THIRD OF THE PLATE IS OCCUPIED BY a grey-stain wall, a clerk's pulpit, a high stool and a sapajou considering a sizeable book of what look to be dried flowers. To assist the viewer the monkey has lifted the far or right side of the ledger; furthermore, his head is inclined towards that page. With one finger of his left hand he presses to the desktop a limp, simple enough plant with a few pale roots, but with two loops in the middle of the stalk. The plant on the desk matches that affixed to the page under which there are some careful-looking cuneiform shapes to represent writing.

He has given me no hat or garment to identify my profession. A flower collector? I always thought they used a squat, little press with a corkscrew twist and sheets of specially soft paper to receive the moisture and colour of the squeezed plant, and there is no sign of that. It would depend on how amateur the collector is? Possible, but I still do not know what I am supposed to be doing with the unpressed item, only that it does not look fresh. Am I identifying it? Or am I comparing it to an already dried example, seeking a better specimen for the collection? Or wistfully considering the relationship between a plant plucked a day or so ago and the long-dried? Other possibilities. A herbalist musing on infusions. An apothecary thinking on properties and poisons – those loops are freakish. Parasitical in origin? Or perhaps the two plants are there simply out of a convenient sense of symmetry. In any case I am not attending to my Duchess and the title does not, I think, refer to any of my capabilities.

Forget Emperors and peacocks and moths. The wings have left her head, become feathered, taken to her back.

I did not at first appreciate that he had borrowed the wings from the guacamayo. I had become used to the taxidermist's closed version. Besides, those wings in the engraving are not arm substitutes, they issue from around her shoulderblades and are fully extended – something the guacamayo rarely did and not at that angelic or crucified angle.

She is not so much flying as hanging, her down-pointed slippers just off the floor, her expression all disbelief and delight, her hands raised, her fingers apart, her legs tensed and stretched.

Look closer. Her eyes are wide, her pupils pointed. Those are her canines snagging on her lower lip. It makes her look feather-brained as well. Her dress I never saw – it is over-ribboned, has a large bow on either side of the thighs with a humbug stripe. Yellow and black? At least satinish. Not her normal taste, which though sometimes precious, was never quite so over-charged or prissy.

In technical terms what have we? From the uncooked dinner onwards the engravings were – even in the exception – never simple lines but extraordinarily busy-fingered, full of scored shadows and damp, with more marks to the inch than any piece of needlework.

32

ON A LAPDOG'S DEATH

———

AL MORIR

UN PERRILLO FALDERO

SHOWS DUCHESS AND HOUSEKEEPER EMBRACING in an upstairs cloister while a capuchin monkey looks back at the viewer with another walnut in his hands. My attitude is one of having been rattling or weighing it. I have a slightly off-centre wide-eyedness. Surprise? At what? The artist would have been in the air. If interest, it looks cool and of the briefest. It certainly is not piety. His haste? Or are we both pointedly interrupted sceptics?

My Duchess's face is entirely hidden behind the old woman's headgear. The whole embrace is very clothy – he has even given them a non-existent back-cloth – all clothes and shawls and hunched drapes and the only human flesh on show is the housekeeper's blurred profile, more nap-worn than tearful, and my Duchess's right hand gripping her aged servant's shoulder. The fingers are taut but it is not a tight grip; the clutch has stayed.

There are a few other matters; the old lady has recuperated her belt – one small key is missing – and my Duchess's right shoe heel is raised.

But there is no indication whatsoever of the circumstances of the death.

A calendar of seasons, the howling of kitchen mutts. On heat, the raisin and curl bitch was treated as a nun. Doors were secured, dogs turfed outside but, by a surprising oversight – though surely nothing to do with that missing key on the belt – a route from another courtyard was forgotten and there came bursting through not dun hackles but a small, overheaded bulldog, his badger abandoned, his bandy legs working furiously to get up the stairs.

The sight of this extraordinary duo – the lapdog demure but willing and the incompetent white bulldog thrusting at air, belly, leg-joint – sent my Duchess into hiccups of laughter. Thoughts of possible offspring almost choked her. The goddaughter was less indulgent, and tossed liquid – cold tea I think – not at the heaving and ineffectual hindquarters but at the bulldog's face. Jowls shook, he growled but instead of sinking his teeth into a black ankle, he blinked and went for me. Shrieking at his stupidity, alarmed by his jaws, I thrashed down a walnut, hit him on the head and went up a column. That nut rolled lazily with a lip-click crack. The dog began to bark at a sapajou and a stone tree.

The bitch was scooped up and locked up; the barker was dragged by the collar back to the crane and civet. He looked – and you should think of his paws sliding on the flagstones but from time to time slipping into a rollicking trot – proud of himself.

I clambered up to the roof and then went along and round to the artist. Though not unfriendly he chose to keep working – on the previous etching of my levitating Duchess. I felt uncomfortably sleepy, blinked, stretched my face. He had the air of someone fastidiously chiaving on. And I realised that what I felt was nausea. The effect of that slobber and bark? It did not matter.

I retired again to the roof and looked out over the Doñana. I was weary of waiting. For what? That there would be a mate for me? I no longer believe. My sexual interest wanes a little more each moon. Where once my muscles tightened, my sight sharpened and power pushed out of my fur, now a thrifty little moan escapes me. Moon on water, ripples disappearing into stone. Then no moan, no new moon.

For eating in its locked room the carelessly left remains of someone's meal – quail bones I think – the wretched lapdog was to receive a little burial and a small tombstone. It died painfully, whining and retching for many hours.

Please note that it was he who picked up the walnut and who always revived the guacamayo with its long mobile tail. It is me who thinks of stuffed poses and lapidary inscriptions and who marvels at the casualty rate round my Duchess.

33

THE PYRAMID

EL PIRAMIDE

COMES WITH AN *ACARTONADO* OR CARDBOARD look, caused by the straight sweeps of an acid- dipped brush and by the shape of the building; it does not rise to an Egyptian apex, but is a series of reducing boxes with small, cupped terminals – acorns – at the corners. There is an external staircase. The night is pale grey, the pyramid paler, the full moon – to the right – paler still.

It is here, I think, that I should mention my Duchess's artist's way with letters. Having square-circled the contents, beginning conventionally, one side, two sides, but then twitching the paper and continuing round the edges up to four lines deep but rarely in order so that the tail end of some words was elongated and twisted up and down and with some lines numbered to provide help to the recipient, he then folded and set up the paper as a small box. It stayed like that until ready to go off whereupon, with two sonorous thumps, he'd flatten the letter into something more conventional. Relationship? It was she who mentioned correspondence, he who started to catch up on his mail. His table became strewn — though not piled – with insecure cubes.

The pyramid forms the background to an arid, stone-strewn landscape devoid of any plant in which round, not a fire but a flat rock, my Duchess's goddaughter, sapajou and housekeeper sit. They might, from their hunch, be playing cards but there are none visible – nor dice, nor sheep's knuckles. The foursome is completed by my Duchess at her blowsiest. She is not squatting like us. Propped up on a cushion she is reclining, all pleated silk, dust and gleam, with her head directed at the rock table but her eyes sliding towards the pyramid. That Peacock moth has settled on her hair again. I do not know if we are sharing her amusement or she, as a sideline, ours. The housekeeper is marzipan smirk and crack, the goddaughter a cowlish O, that lower lip silvery; I may be cracking my knuckles, am certainly extracting pleasure or oil from my hands. All look as if we are holding something, my Duchess one-handed. What? *Very* small cards? Or would coins make better sense or fortune? Or what do you say to tinkers' mirrors?

Very well. I may have misunderstood. Judge for yourselves. I am more interested in the relation, if any, between this engraving and the last of their picnics. Why did he make such thorough-going changes? Of course there is no such pyramid anywhere here but the small customs-guards block we passed has pineapple terminals and stairs to the roof. The housekeeper never came out but carefully supervised the food and drink we took. It was midday in August in the south of Spain, not a moonlit night. Through tor grass and timothy, bugloss, blue rosemary and resinous cistus, brushing up a tapestry of scents, placid horses carried us to a cluster of holm oak. My Duchess wore cheerful, old-fashioned clothes with a short, sleeveless and buttonless waistcoat embroidered in lichen white (*aspicilia*) and lichen orange (*caloplaca*), and a large straw hat decorated with Spanish oyster plant. A daytime moth, a male oak eggar, fluttered by her head. Her goddaughter pricked her fingers tugging an acorn from a kermes oak, bled, wore a white bandage on her left hand.

Morose and listless our artist sat at picnic. It was he who found the day slow and dull and sickening, she who encouraged him. Plates clinked. A lizard rustled. Even a chameleon finally moved. But he was unsavable, could not hear, barely looked up in the hot drouse and drone of insects. He ate though, stolidly chewing, stickily swallowing.

I have a problem in that I have a better memory of his scratches than of some of the events in the affair. Did he have in mind the night when he lay across her bed, his feet still on the floor, draped back as it were, grave and limp and grey-blue? I found a long horn beetle investigating a corner. The moon was full and I shinned up to consider the inscrutable stains on it. Later I was surprised to see the beetle being carried off by an undertrain of ants. Had I been staring moonwards longer than I thought? My Duchess and her artist looked to be sleeping but then, with the sliding sound of dry sheets, she laughed and kissed him. And no, between long horn beetle and glum chameleon were various days. Surely there was a new moon after the pyramid picnic?

34

THE SENIOR LADY

LA DAMA MAYOR

IS MY DUCHESS DRESSED AS FOR A RELIGIOUS procession – though not as she was for *Nuestra Señora del Mar* on the twenty-third of August, with sash and many decorations. He has first drawn her body, then dressed her; the effect is of shiftless velvet and lace, black scorings and leafy tendrils and a patchiness that contrasts with her filagreed fan and a mantilla more air than material that is almost down to a train. There are two areas, between threadbare and scratch, on her upper belly and the outside of her right thigh that show his procedure clearly. She is, that is, less dressed than covered over. Given the nature of copper plate I do not know how deliberate this effect is, whether or not this was always his intention or if he changed his mind. Nor can I remember quite when he covered her nakedness. But not long after, a matter of hours. He spent some time on a number of tight-worked rings on her fingers.

The feet, the pose, we have seen before from another angle – in the picture gallery – though her expression, now haughty, is quite new. Here the fan is part of an impatient game involving the other hand – tap and grip. She is not waiting for the processional drum to beat and the Sea Virgin to be hefted but for her goddaughter to attend to something in the small of her back. A meatiness here – the goddaughter is mostly rump – reminiscent of *zíngaras* and pantomime horses. I think the goddaughter arrived with the dress.

I am some sort of beadle; I go in front, in a fur-trimmed three-cornered hat, carrying a short, but ornate staff. I was there when she was naked.

My Duchess enjoyed this etching very much – it was one of the very few she stopped to examine when he was still working through them – but complained he had not shown how her shoes squeezed. Her appearance, unannounced in his rooms, rustle-rush but no knock, startled me almost as much as him. I am not sure if her intention was to single out his skill as a cobbler – the Senior Lady had always worn shoes – or the idealised smallness he had given hers. Her complaint was not spoken; she relied on wince, downward look, restless feet – then lifted the right and waggled it from the knee, toes rapidly, shin swinging.

Our artist blinked. He bowed. He had a grandiose, very sharp-eyed concern for his pride. She lowered her foot to prise off the other shoe and show him the weals it had made. His head remained bowed but he emitted a startling grunt – a mix of pain and relief, like an old man finally easing his bowels. Heel to weal, she rubbed and smiled.

I had been observing this clowning pair from the floor under the paint table but moved smartly to a chair when he swung round and picked up a tube of paint, uncapped it, squeezed up a little worm of vermilion, and showed it against an easelled canvas. He looked round at her. Leer? Or was that confirmation he wanted? She smiled wider, benignly, clapped hands twice and sent for her shoes with the red bows; having done that she gave him a wry, formal nod and offered me her index finger to shake. Uncomfortable, looking away, I reached up and tugged.

Had she gone to make another barefoot tour of the place? Given the circumstances I did not follow her but sat and watched him sit. Elbows out, hands on his beefy thighs, back hunched, heels off the ground, he was in the pose of a jiggler but kept still. When the red bow shoes arrived – on a cushion, on a cushion – he set the left one on a stool and showed it to his palette. The right he did not leave alone but, with the gesture of a careful pervert, paletted cushion and shoe a little further away. Content, he returned to the easel and briskly toned his vermilion. Compared silk and paint. Frowned. Suddenly, with a look at me, he imitated the badger's rumbling bark and its shoulder roll; equally suddenly he broke off to bend and smell, with every sign of lung-filling relish, the instep.

My expression? I imagine extremely cautious. Scratch-tracing my left eyebrow made him laugh – ha! Why? My Duchess had slippery feet, often washed, some crushed at the toes, with an incipient bunion on the right big joint.

The smell? Sour milk when it is plumping, cinnamon biscuit, a little stale, a little sweated.

35

MONO RECONOCIENDO

A UNA DUQUESA ECHADA

MONKEY EXAMINING A RECLINING DUCHESS? AN impertinent title? and/or clumsy? I cannot be recognising her. Reconnoître is too far-fetched. And despite the suggestion of a doctor lurking in the title the engraving contains no medical or scientific paraphernalia to assist the examination.

There is no sign of fatigue or illness. My Duchess is solidly asleep, her face turned almost full to the viewer – in practice a mite too far for her neck to bear without cracking. A sapajou sits on her naked chest, left leg resting on and partially covering her right breast, and with some lippy concentration stares at her upper left lid which his clawed right index finger is about to reach. Monkey cautiously exploring sleeping Duchess?

Am I going to poke, scratch or lift? I'd say the last.

She and I – all of me, her head and top trunk – fill the frame – except for a patch at the upper left-hand corner. I mean I look as if I were fitting myself into a tight box. He has made me too large. She would have woken. Perhaps to counteract this she has a cut-stone look – not simply in the regularised face; that breast bears no sign, no tuck, no impression, caused by my gripping toes. Her hair has been done with a firm, twitchy point, crinkle by crin, off her face. Her hairs enhance the softness of my fur – though he has given me what looks like a wet patch – a sweat gland? – at the hip.

The upper-left corner is scrappy. He started something which he then scored out but he did not bother to disguise the scoring or change it into something else. I think – I cannot be certain – it is the shadow of a moth. Perhaps it *is* the moth.

I am not good at speculation, but if the reader has put in a fraction of the effort I have used to sustain scratch and image, there should be no surprise when I say that, the visual faculty relaxed, other senses waft in – in my case fitfully and with brevity enough to mean I must trace them back to their setting and circumstances. I admit a certain longing, a false exoticism buoys them up. Examples? Hearing naturally. Touch as well. But I have most in mind my senses of colour and smell – blood-red, blood-sweet.

It is then, reader, factual to describe the affair as fitting between two menstrual turns of the moon, the first period generously shared, the second, via a delicate but unanswerable note, indisposed and private. Compare this engraving with the meal and napkins he made of the fifth or his swagger and bounce (through 6, 7, 8, 9) to begin again with a guacamayo- and capuchin-decorated farthingale. Consider a moment: was he offended by her new-found delicacy, annoyed enough by his exclusion to pubic the hair of her head? Was he mocking his own desire – to have my access to my Duchess but his distended interest? Oh, I see copper sneers. That tail of mine, an inferior extension right enough, is sufficiently prehensile to sound the underside of her breast. Yet he has made that a chill, marmoreal bub. Tail-stethoscope on a statue. And I look insidious, like nightmare's jockey. But whose?

And from where came that wretched moth? Why did he have need of a moth? Moths and monkeys do not mix with marble – nor marble with hair and blood. When what he wanted was to listen to the chambers of her heart. Absurd. Scratch. Sasosasosu. Blacken that moth.

In her business room my out-of-sorts Duchess wrote letters or, rather, having rubbed her hands hard enough to heat them, she ambled back and forward, not dictating but sometimes, usually belatedly, choosing another word in her secretary's suggested sentences. She sighed. She sat. With one eye closed she considered the first of his draughts, shook her head, rose, gave it back, strolled, winced. His prompt offer to return later she turned down but left nothing for him to work on. She took a turn or two about the room, then absently paused to scratch the top of my head – a gesture left over from the lapdog – found energy and charitably halved a macaroon for me. I had, in consequence, little choice but to leave. Did she say anything? A murmur, something vague. The oversweet bits I tossed down for the peahen who blinked, considered, clucked – and rejected. Out in the courtyard the goddaughter sat on one side of the stone tank, stirring the water with a finger. The cat lay opposite her watching the fish while enjoying the warmth and showing an ear-twitching, lid-stretching tension between appetite – those gleaming, lip-slipped fangs – and portly sleep. I understood the goddaughter was pushing her finger through her own reflected lips. Brackish, cool. I snorted. I jumped up and swung round, pattering along to the artist. He had already begun on his next perspectives. The candle he had lit was more for warning than for light. Where he was was as dark as a cave. But contrast a moment – I did – thick parchment and ink, plate and brilliant scratches.

36

UP

ARRIBA

SHOWS MY OLD COMPANION, THE SHE-ASS, WITH her four hoofs linearly arranged on a tightrope – slack as his jowl-line – between two gondolier capstan poles. A sapajou in a ridiculous circus hat calls attention to the trick, wears a public grin, a bullfighter's trophy hands. But down on the ground his heels are up and his toes have begun sidling away from responsibility or danger.

If you look closely, the rope to the right behind the donkey has begun to untwine; her ears are down, her nostrils clamped, her tail is between her legs, but her eye has overlarge lashes and her lips are those of a simperer.

This is, without doubt, amusing but am I wrong to think that the artist was solely occupying himself – was he marking time, practising his hand while he waited as much as giving vent to his irritation? The candle wavered. Slowly, without apparent attention – he seemed to be looking at me – he made those poles barbers'.

37

THE HOOK

———

EL ANZUELO

I AM FISHING FROM DUNGEON WALLS IN NEAR darkness. Some faint light fed down shows me sat on the edge of a dark pit with a rod (a sapling is that?), a line and a key, reader, in place of hook or for that matter bait. On my head I have a crown of bay leaves of the kind seen on neo-classical marble busts of prizewinners.

Dogfish? A heap of snarling mutts, coils of eyes, jaws and spines, rises out of the black base. It is topped by a white bulldog who looks to have snapped and missed. Not quite elegant enough to be snakelike; the tangle is abrupter, more haunched, those tails yelp-tucked. Stop. This is a muscled, white-tipped dog-wave breaking against the wall.

My expression – it *is* difficult to see – is as if saintlily waiting for the afflatus, ignorant of the growl and leap below.

Dog-pit and key? Dungeon-pier and white-face poet? What does all this mean? Why so grandiose in his shadows? So violent? The matter is bluntly etched, as troubled as a nightmare. But where – through pyramids and toads, snakes and keys – is the cause, the hinge?

For goodness sake. See 21, at the centre.

Sitting beside him I had the impression of a metal book shutting. Pressed sapajou? No, no. Pressed dragonfly? No. I saw a miserable substitute: a body drawn with black ink and fallen petals pushed into the place of wings. Where? On his writing desk where old flowers had turned their water brown; he leant over and took morose advantage of petals and paper.

Did I ever bite him? Feel his shin bone with my teeth?

I considered the insect body, lifted a curled and faded wing. He put down his pen and watched. I rolled the old pink petal to make a decollated snail shell, let it go. I looked up. He was still waiting. I brushed the other wings away, smearing the still-wet ink.

Our artist nodded briefly and began the next plate. I tried to rub the ink off my fingers – a disagreeable sensation – and remembered, crawling from the courtyard tank, a tiny, six-legged albino homunculus, as slow as a large-eyed chameleon but jerky. I blinked at an impression of white pipe clay stuck with matches, apparently wet bald but, seen very close, with sparse, even, colourless bristles. (Is there an element of ink that smells like clay?) Its nether and under regions were all soaked leaf tangle and sodden sac from which I thought the creature was struggling to extricate itself. The middle legs shift, the mouth works – a glaucous old man at a biscuit – but there is a sudden flop, the excrescence drops, uncurls, becomes tail, tripling the total length, making the homunculus thorax and head.

The tail stiffens. But where are the wings? Slimy tucks, viscous as snail-run moss. Slowly, eyes bulge, wings twitch and begin to expand.

The dragonfly is defenceless for at least two hours until its double wings are stretched taut and ready.

38

¡QUE OFICIO!

IS THIS MY TRADE OR HIS SKILL? I AM PORTRAYED with my legs and feet far apart, a dreadfully uncomfortable squat-straddle apparently explained by what I have under each set of toes; a plump common toad to the right, the head of a snake to the left. On my heels, my sinews stretched, my back hunched, in dungeon dark again, I don't think I have just landed after an heroic jump.

The toad is quite accurately and wartily done, its lids almost closed, its mouth open, but the gaping snake, with the markings of the local viper, is over-headed, too short, too thick and ends slackly like an empty sock.

My elbows are tight together in my hollowed stomach, my hands clasped as I worry at or gnaw on a dry peach stone.

Why?

Did he believe toads have a poisonous bite? Surely it is the other way round, that some, when bitten, can secrete poison. And who bites toads? I quite enjoy watching them. They have no tenacity and are easily deflated.

Am I supposed to be keeping the reptiles apart?

Or am I saving the toad from the snake?

Why should a sapajou do either?

Let us grant that vipers are dangerous, especially when stepped on – anywhere, that is, except just behind the head. So?

Well, am I here the catcher caught with the two reptiles secured but at the limit of my stretch and unable to move without danger?

Surely not if I let go of the inoffensive toad? Even picking the amphibian up – having abandoned the peach stone – I'd have leg and speed to rescue us both.

Then what *is* my *oficio*? Reptile catcher? Without my cleft stick? Faced with a poisonously disgusting choice? Is that it? That reptiles are conventionally repulsive?

The expression is blunt, even powerful, but somehow I find it obscure – or rather I suspect obscurity to be the point of it. He is here more interested in expressing than telling.

And just look at the last detail, surely not an oversight. My sexual parts have been excised, furred over. Was this aesthetic – given the inelegance of the straddle – or compositional, to avoid the triangular head of a triangle – or a deliberate emasculation?

Imagine: behind your unsuspecting, reading head – a sudden thunderous handclap. Ha! Exactly. In

39

I MEASURE

ESTIMO

THE FIRST SIGHT WORKS ON THE HEARING; THE engraving is a deafener.

A hinge-cracking shove – ah, the pain in this thrust-open door! The exultant misery.

Is there fraud? ¿*Timo*?

There is certainly displacement – a dark ghost of a reflection shows the artist in the title, but there is no plumbline, pencil or proportion. His thumb is in his fist, his fist is furiously closed and his squint is all glower. That hand and arm are shown twice: the arm of a colossus, reflected in a mirror tilted above the dining pair, juts out into the etching from the left foreground, not so much over-muscled as rough-sculpted. The stony fist is punch-tight.

From under the table, bursting towards the right foreground, a sapajou flees, all jack-crossed limbs, feet higher than hands, howl-hollow lips and fear. If you look closely, if you look past my lips – more fluty and simian than capuchin monkey – there are unexplained whitish stains on my fur. His startling entry caused me to be hit by a slop of rennet, white but not gelatinous stuff that crawled down my fur and sank through to chill my skin. The artist has removed that spoon and that bowl. Curdled oversight? Or was he suggesting some one-sided, half-life business?

The table is a miracle of rancidness, lace like draped, sectioned lungs, plates like lead pools, implements twisted, the grapeskins retractable, a candelabra contorted but the shrinking and back flutter of the candleflames barely begun; they tilt a couple of degrees to the left.

The mirrored artist is between and over the couple. My Duchess is carefully lit. Her companion, the replete bully-bag with one drooping eye, barely obtrudes from the shadows as a jacketed wax-flow on the way down to congealing.

She looks directly back at the measurer, her hair and headdress cobwebs or at least a threaded vaporousness, her eyes large and cool. There is no hint that the males around her – melting, fleeing or in a paroxysm of discovery and recrimination – are anything but strange to her. She has merely paused – her left hand is not shown – in shaking drops from her right hand into the fingerbowl. At least that is my impression; she is about to raise her fingers to acquire momentum for the shake, was just enjoying the feel of the tepid water.

In any case, he romanticises; let me be less melodramatic and more prosaic. That waxworks third-party certainly existed but formally enough, after a stiff letter of presentation. A slight fellow, tight-jawed, flisty-eyed, bald, his remaining hair short and soft and brushed towards a wide, wedge-shaped centre-parting, he was an official or officer of some kind in a tight uniform and boots – a surveyor or an architect checking coastal towers? – with a dignity prudish and thin lips plosive at her attentions. Did they ride their horses together? I no longer recall. She helped him to dishes while passing tidbits down to me by his gleaming boots. He sat with his knees together, hen-toed, heels up, a position for cramps – not that of a libertine or a pleasured guest – to go with his nervy smirk.

More. The supper was not a tutorial but a seminar, fourteen places at three tables in the shape of a U, five each side and a base, note, of four. The base our artist halved, and those side tables, the outflankers and their occupants, he swept aside – though his own place had been set at the extreme right. Where had he been?

He did indeed thrust out his arm and grip his hidden thumb. But there are other observations to make. He made the officer start and drop his spoon and though the dropper had a large dangling napkin he thought instantly of his uniform, and flicked – the spoon hit me and skittered across the floor towards the artist.

Nor did my Duchess stay mabbishly still; she jumped to her feet and snarled – a powerful combination of grinding teeth and whisper – ¡Tengo hacha! I have an axe! – just as the posset touched my skin. I screamed. I fled. The artist watched my progress across the floor and gave his hidden thumb one last squeeze. I was snatched up and napkin-dried. My Duchess let out a ha! more indignant-incredulous than amused and dropped back into her chair. The spoon stayed on the floor. My Duchess grew angrier at the artist's ghost, the open door, blamed the spoon, had it picked up – and I found I had become more swaddled than wrapped. My Duchess showed her teeth and resumed her hostess role though I, who had been placed in the crook of her right arm and tightly tucked in, could feel that her right leg kept time to a vigorous half-second pulse.

Cha! Freed of damask, along flagged corridors, up stone stairs – somehow I was expecting noise. In retrospect, absurd. Supper was over, there was nobody about that wing and my scented Duchess and her guests had withdrawn to another for sweetmeats and music; she found distraction in those resonant minglings of thrum and murmur and the watery drop of notes, I hate those fingers squeaking on strings and chords and the dull underclick of keys.

Perhaps what I expected was the visual evidence of past noise, things strewn, wood broken? Or was that just an impression from the silence? Was it damp? Oyster-stone musty? No. Here were no salmon mousse smells, no *fruit glacé*. A cobweb trembled, giving off a gleam like saliva. I scooted along and ducked into his bedroom.

What did I find there? The desisted preliminaries of despair and packing; some clothes piled on the campaign bed, several pairs of shoes lined up. His bath had not been emptied. The sodden sponge barely broke the surface of the water. A chair had been used for a trio of jackets and – wait, yes, I think the horsehair leaking from the sheep's-skull eye sockets had been digited back. With the hatcheted thumb?

I found him in the second room (see letters and oils). He had some packed here too – a bound bunch of brushes, a thicker stack of canvasses, less jar lids about – and was sitting at his letter table glued in gloom, right hand gripping his jaw, left hand limp on a blank sheet of paper. If he wanted to marvel at the difference in his hands he could have pressed out his palmprints on acid and metal. Would that have burnt him? Very well.

I blinked. There was no pen or pencil with which to write a letter or record the mitt. Did he think the left hand had a separate life of its own? Had failed to blossom like the right? Or had failed to act as a restraint? Sometimes, particularly when my lids and brows are sticky, I find that my tongue quickens and tutting the back of my front teeth sounds like clicking – a little air, a fat tonguetip and saliva are unpleasantly like a stick on spokes. I snort-sneezed and jumped up on to the table. His eyes shifted to me without obvious signs of pleasure or, for that matter, recognition. He did, however, ease his face, first with fingers, then without. He sighed. His features resettled. His paper hand never moved.

For a while I watched this immobile item; then I lifted his index finger and let go. It sank back.

I am not sure – my action had not meant to be a request, I had been mildly intrigued by a hand playing dead – but he exhaled loudly and resignedly and turned it over, flop. There was no stretching of the palm, the fingers curled, thumb and index nearly touching, the whole resting on three knuckles, mostly the two smallest. He was morosely considering the foot of the nearest easel, working his lips as if very patiently trying to suck a bit of apple skin from between his teeth.

Brows up, I tilted and peered at the hand. His lips slowed, became more cuddie, but nothing happened. The hand remained still. I looked closer. But there was nothing obviously in it, certainly nothing edible. The palm was teeming with the usual cuts and breaks and there was a kind of chain pattern at the base of the fingers and on the principal lines. These lines were linked, made a stylised W – or from his position an even more stylised M – with curves crossing some of them like those arcs made by drawing compasses. There was a large star or asterix under the third finger but there was nothing else of much note or that different from any other well-fleshed, fifty-year-old male hand, though the small finger seemed mildly twisted inwards; broken and badly-set? . . . and I became aware that he was watching me. But what did he think? I was merely disappointed. With the slowness of a pedant he demonstrated his opposable thumb.

Did he object to my prosaic additions – my quibbles, his swept-away tables? He grunted, flexed the exhibit and with the nails of the other hand crackled face bristle. He grimaced.

'*Vete*,' he said, absently sawing at an itch in the dip between lower lip and chin.

And so I went.

40

THE MONKEY'S MOTHER

MADRE DEL MONO

HE MUST HAVE DONE AFTER THE INCONCLUSIVE palmistry, having strolled through to the third room. His revenge on me is beyond all reason. Nothing in his dreary eyes had prepared me. The engraving is worse than a nightmare.

A trio of imbeciled faces, features veal-caul and fish-roe, sit behind and to the right of a fire. Despite the shadows and the haggery of clothes and squat, my Duchess and her goddaughter are easily recognisable, like hastily-prepared actors. They flank the main personage, whose face wears a replete expression as if a toad had recently sat over her flat nose and toothless mouth and done her the honour of a fart – the nether-clotted housekeeper.

It is she – her foisted face, turned proudly to the viewer, is almost twice the size of the others – that holds the stick. Some bellows, yes, bellows – with a studded, pseudo-Moorish pattern – poke out from the shadows and skirts. A sapajou's head, a monstrous chestnut with dandelion hair, stares wide-eyed from between the clothy hips of housekeeper and goddaughter.

Light (little) and heat (suffused) issue from the same source, a ground-fire with an ovoid hem of large, smooth stones.

My mother has been skinned, her innards spilt out (where? in the shadows?), the housekeeper's stick rammed through the ripped loins and snugly centred in the skull. The tail has been wound round the wood to prevent it dropping into the flames, the long arms folded out on a cross stick and trussed at the elbows. The legs have proved no problem. They have adopted, with sinew-tightening heat, the stiff spread of the rabbit.

Those lipless teeth – what care he has taken! to fix the perspective, the relationship of gum to each exposed tooth! And the eye! Stop – *do* the lids really peel off with the skin? The eye resembles an over-cooked mussel – soft rupture, webbish tendon and a mucousless hole for the pupil. More black; a deposit of carbon on the flap of skin hanging from the rib cage and a patch on the bare skull. Her fingers are stiff but closing, her feet still raw, still cold.

The heat makes me conscious of the form of my own eyes and the liquid that lets them slide. I am forgetting the bellows here and his earlier ability when I was served up to add salt when there was none.

Yet who could compose and etch this – not swift enough for a fit, not cross-eyed enough for rage? I'll tell you. A gnawed, black, ignoble ghost, a deaf, thick-fingered, pouch-eyed dramatist of betrayal.

But where was the betrayal? If not in him? For surely what my Duchess did was to take refuge in actions, play in them, avoid them – but provide little comment and no moral. Her excitement came from the opposition of words and actions, the feints, the precisions, the costume padding, the unsaid; without a form of words her actions did not bind her, not in her little oyster-stone palace.

I am aware. This last is my description of relative laws, not the expression of his pain. Nor mine.

I? I'd have made peach stones of his shins.

And having slaughtered my mother? He walked and struck statuesque poses in his darkened suite of rooms. Was he acting only for me? Or for another, better version of himself, with less belly and sag? And what kind of statue faces a corner and hunches?

Aaaah! Have you never, male reader, felt like uprooting yourself? Mm? No whirr, no iridescence; the sudden grip of thick blood. There are some creatures so beautiful they cause anguish. Have I got that right, the agony swollen, the striving central? A gorged mace, a trembling fist. The apprehension is mine, the desire, jerkily deliquescing into sentiment, is one-sided – a product of my furrowed little mind. There is no relation. Do not, if you wish to avoid being disgusting, draw any similarity between his situation (curdled there, furiously fermented here) and mine (startled, blink-impotent petdom). Does self-abuse excuse vindictive despair? Clutched and pale, it only follows.

Even so, I ask myself – what is the link between the sexual urge and dragonflies? Ahh, I had it here a moment ago; a needle of colour, an enchanting shimmer. Nothing *at all* to do with fire or the arsonist cooked.

I shivered. He sighed and buttoned. At no time after taking measure did our heroic artist go to bed, in the sense of clambering up and on to a feather-stuffed horizontal plane to sleep. As well as posing, he engraved, painted, packed, pottered – and sat in a wooden chair. There he rubbed his eyes, groaned, dropped off, grunted and glowered. For how long? One night, one day, another night. At the end of that second vigil, just before sunrise on the thirty-first of August, he and his carriage were to trickle away. The silence was only broken by slow axle-creak and the snorting of horses allowed to pull but not to trot. A deaf man's respect for night peace? Possibly he was just grudging.

Except for one brief excursion he remained entirely in his rooms for some thirty to thirty-two hours. During them he executed four etchings (do not, I beg you, forget 21 and 40, Saint George and The Monkey's Mother), finished off a portrait in oils (the red bow), listed (half-heartedly) materials used and remaining, wrapped up his notebooks, titled and numbered the final arrangement of his engraved skirting board, before he re-hatted (candle-brim in his hand) and, at least affecting the chill of fatigue, black-cloaked himself and abandoned first rooms, then cloisters and last, palace and Sanlúcar.

Let me concentrate not on his final doings but the pall on them. Was it the additional effect of his charcoaled walls and shadow-vaulted ceiling? But after the shock of the evisceration and the acid-speckled copper, I found not so much a suggestibility in that middle room as a miasma. The stamina of his offence! I tend to forget slights but he thickened his, as with pearl barley, with a perverse gusto. That was an ossuary dark, grainy as a black-stained dog-day sail with flecks of bonemeal. An unoccupied chair creaked. The untended easel sighed. I heard something seethe like very hot oil, smelt a waft of wasp-rotted apples. From under a table, clasping the cross-strut, I saw him stop work, slump back, knee over chair arm, uncork linseed and sniff, unimpressed.

Perhaps his dismissive aplomb misled me and I mistook despair for arrogance. But the flickering light on the glistening bottle reminded me of a pair of white porcelain monkeys with human hands, human calves and monkey's feet (with spectacular hawkish claws) performing an endless jig. Their headhair and whiskers rather leonine, their clothes rustic-swain – a raised tambourine for the hatless one, a flute for the plumed tricorn – they gave off a repulsive gleam; there was no light that showed them without bright blind spots, no angle that did not expose virulent, glazed rents. Nine inches of contorted, reflecting white. At least my Duchess had the grace or caution when she saw my reaction to have them removed, placed in bags, stored away in a cupboard.

He? He drank his way slowly through two bottles of Burgundy, via a glass that he first buffed up with fastidious care but which became clouded by finger and lip prints and acquired, on the under slope, a trace of grey-blue paint and in the bowl a deposit of syrup, crystals and lees. He began with a pensative sup, then a slow rinsing of teeth and gums finishing with a liver-twisting wince.

Around the time his tongue began to feel dry and tender she tied, first with a ribbon, then with more practical document tape, a small note to my tail. A tail only looks suitable, even a collar is better, but as soon as I made to unpick the tape, she stopped me.

'No, no. Así es, así.' Like that.

In consequence I went between them with my tail in my hand, lolloping along, three-limbed on the flagstones. Our artist heard my entry, showed me his stained tongue in a tremendous, noisy yawn – note, please, the pinkish tape, the purplish taste-buds – but saw nothing and I had to wait for him to scratch his upper belly and wipe his eyes before making my tail snake. It is only partly prehensile, lacks vigour and suppleness but I got the message to rattle; I caught it behind the head, jumped back and shook it. The artist blinked, grunted, banged the letter table.

'Hup!'

I complied, looked off while his thick fingers slowly tackled the knot in the tape – what is the opposite of affably? The relationship between his nearly nailless digits – he had a rim of swollen flesh lagooning short flat-mooned horn – and his indistinct, curse-toned mutter was hoary-clear. Fingertips licked, tape untied, paper unfolded . . . I looked round, he looked back . . . I used a leg to get at an itch behind my ear.

'Ya, ya,' he said.

I smoothed my tail. And the message? He ripped it up without passion but very small and with surprising precision. Then he took unlit candle to lit candle to parchment. Though burnt in a bowl the contents can still be deduced. The paper flared up – *did* he feint at warming his hands or was that just a hasty attempt to correct overspill? – and I retreated at once, sped out and back to my Duchess, the first stretch, I was more distracted than I knew, on three limbs again, my right eye twitching to get rid of the image of that flame. It was only when squirming in her lap that I appreciated the link between her perfume and the message.

'Nothing?'

Avoiding her eyes I held out my hand for a reward. She chose a nut, dusted it, but in the act of giving suddenly grabbed me and tumbled me about. I had no reply on my person but her hands ran over my body and tail . . . she stopped, nodded and had her hand scratch dog-style between my ears. I prefer under the chin and showed her. She sighed exasperation, used her forearm to push me off.

41

THE TROOP

LA TROPA

IS THE FIRST AND LAST OF ITS KIND, AND I ADMIT, troubles me. Those were busy, broken hours. I have turned my eyes round too much, been too much in darkness, scurried up and down too many cloistered passages. Even so, my doubt shames and irritates me. But no matter if I squeeze hard on my lids – did I see some earlier version? but when? on paper? – two pairs of artists and Duchesses effortlessly co-exist. They are a twosome that swivels like a compartment in my Duchess's writing desk, so well balanced by the cabinetmaker it feels lubricated, a quarter-circular segment that skips to and fro at a touch. It is only the angle that changes.

The Duchess, naked, sitting on a heavy wooden chair, with one foot on one knee, is now rather blowsy and double-chinned. Her head is cocked, her smile sleepy and ironic. The main difference is that the two versions of her are facing different corners. Hinged at the spine? My memory prefers to slide along a trapezium.

Our artist is likewise devoid of clothes, but discreetly – though I have seen him like a beached seaslug and here it is the thigh that swells. Potteringly, he addresses a canvas on an easel. But is he to the left of the frame in cock-docked (*pito-quito*) profile – or to the right, showing more pale old man's bum cheek in my gloom? In neither case is there anything on the canvas but in both he has a palette and wields a treacle-laden brush, with the gleam of wet fur. I repeat, I regret I do not know which swivel to take. And the capuchin? He is everywhere. To suggest multiple possibilities? A riot? At any rate I am well done, carefully done, whereas they are much sketchier, scratch, dab and a starred last melon.

Did he mean *tropo* not *tropa*, trope not troop? Please note that I am not, as it were, integrated into the engraving. I am not perched on an easel or chair or hanging from any drape. I am instead a sort of frieze and am always given what looks like a dancing master's stick. *Monsieur le singe* again? *Pas du tout.* I defy gravity but there is no sign of an eugenic ceiling; I am upright all round. This is decoration. There are too few of me to be the markings of a clock, too many to represent each of his weeks there.

How many are there? Let's count. 1) I curtsey with the stick in both hands above my head. 2) I seem to be conducting again, finger raised, with a very large baton. 3) I swagger, commissioned militarily, with a curled tail. 4) With stick vertical and back straight I bend at the knee to pick up a coin – or a lady's pearl –

from the floor. 5) Stick horizontal, elbows out, I pirouette. 6) With stick-pointer, stick-writing-instrument, I look to be lecturing on a faint patch of sand. 7) A very fastidious gentleman, I am trying to remove a slimy leaf from the tip of my walking stick without polluting my hands and with the minimum of toe-work. 8) I give a folkloric clodskip, rather flushed with drink, rather short of teeth, as if about to toss the stick above my head.

And the point? Surely you see what I mean about tropes? I am, eight-fold, a margin, an edge. But not quite theatrical. I do not decorate a proscenium arch. Nor am I bookish. There is no pattern and my tails do not link up. The thing is awry. I am, despite the detail, flat, without perspective; they, in spite of their scratch, are with. A parody of understudies? Of prompted loves? I do not know but the reader should not feel surprised that my memory of the engraving makes me feel dislocated. Why? The artist has just shed a smile, some exhalation, mostly throaty agreement, and is on the point of concentrating on the first thick stroke. I am without gravity. Of course with run enough I can skip up the wall and off the ceiling but I cannot stay there. There is no miracle. I cannot fly. I cannot, however swack and sinuous, hang in the air. Wait. Let me retreat a little. Yes, it is like peering through a window at the scene inside, a cut-copper garland of monkeys acts as blinkers or cupped hands, an effect more black than grey that is somehow *alegre* . . . cheerful.

Frowning, I looked round at him. He had exasperatingly quick and radical changes of mood: sarcastic, sullen, apparently euphoric – for the most part privately though even when I was included my dumbness was complicit, my gifts of mime easily misunderstood. He nodded at my hands round my face; but the reaction I saw most was a tooth-grinding smile, followed smartly by indifference, a sup of his wine and a resumption of his business. Well, the engraving was set down. I moved.

Post tail-letter and troop, around half-past eight in the evening – surely the time in the carbonised message, with an 'if otherwise unoccupied' likely – she sent me to do her fetching. I found him jiggling his leg but, shaved and spry, at some business in front of a mirror, from which he turned on me the face of a Japanese devil, prior to clapping his candled-hat (see *The Duchess's Guest*, number 2, here unlit) on his head and veering off at a burly lick to his appointment.

In the din of dusk – the thick chatter of the birds in the four palms, the cat's lazy control of at least one fourth the volume, the raucous, jealous peacock which drowned out drowsy insect drone but not a spasmodic, solitary crick – he did slow down to glare briefly at the courtyard. I wish to make it clear, however, that I preceded him along cloisters and down stairs at *his* pace, except at the end when I ran as a small, furry warning to my Duchess – and to her secretary, the man behind the desk in the corner shadows – she rising as I leapt breastwards.

With me under one arm, she greeted him graciously, he greeted her, removing his hat, kissing over her knuckles while his eyes slid off to the demure man of business. They sat – at either extremity of the desk's leading edge – on light chairs but faced neither the secretary nor each other; she cocked an ear, he an eye, he with his hat on his lap, my Duchess with me. She toyed with and stroked the fur on my head, glanced at him, but missed I think the frequency of his throat clearing – dry gorge, a sticking so polite it was barely audible. Settling up took very few minutes. Note, however, despite his glum jaw and his thumb carefully circling some wax on his hat, his instantaneous negative drawl at one misread sum for an oil portrait and the secretary's immediate bob and blot – huh! – of contrition. I have never properly understood why, when the corner of a sheet of blotting paper is applied to a blob of ink, the black stuff makes upwards in gooseflesh rushes; does it climb over the already saturated stuff or does it push it up? And how upwards? A triangle – or, in this case, a semi-opened fan. Our artist's fingernail picked at beeswax, my Duchess grew conscious of her lips, seemed to find them bloated, spent a couple of seconds with them sucked between her teeth, sour-squeezing them as you might roll a lemon, but then breathed in, smoothed me, felt for my shoulderblades through my fur, used her fingers like arthritic flute stops.

You cannot be in two places at once but knowledge and speed can palliate the deficiency; he was shortly to engrave plates 21 and 42, she, though there was no wind, to bathe her eyes in camomile tea.

No moth-like metaphors or insinuating smiles followed their business. Their energies went into impassive, separate dignities. He ushered her out of the room into the unlit cloister, replaced his unlit, candle-brimmed hat and she, at my first wriggle, let me go. I think – they accompanied each other slowly and politely over the flagstones – that they were easily able to take as read the possibility of future meetings elsewhere and in public. It was too

145

dark for further conversation. Behind her in the courtyard the gardener was drenching plants. The artist bowed and swung round and up the steps. She remained, briefly, pensatively, until she made me out.

'*Basta*,' she said. Enough. She waved me away, almost at once found her lids dry enough to be sore. But when she saw I had not gone she thrust out her jaw and made the shocking, bitter gestures I had in number 18, her pumping hand about the size of my neck. I dropped back, breathed in the scent of watered leaves and wet earth.

Unhatted for supper, in a relative blaze of candlelight, five on the brim, two in sticks, he ate some oily-green leek soup into which he splashed some red wine from his glass, distributing the drops from the bowl and stem, licking the base and then spooning the colours together in a messy whirl, before grinding a small fistful of salted nuts and sprinkling the results over the surface. With the soup he ate *jamón serrano*, bright stuff from black-skinned pigs that I find far too rich, crusty bread and a green olive or two which, having first offered to me, he consumed, all chomp and stolid relish.

Whereas my Duchess – think of the tingling pads of my feet – apart from breaking off a game of piquet with her goddaughter (which she did not resume) for an unfinished glass of muscatel and an almond biscuit, went otherwise supperless. She preferred to hide her head over a steaming infusion – to open her pores rather than to clear catarrh, inspite of her noisy inhalations. What routines she had! Not so much slow as not to be hurried, not so much deliberate as indifferent, not so much slothful as self-absorbed; it was as if her metabolism was already asleep but that

146

the sleep had not yet gravitated to her tending hands. With every brushstroke from her goddaughter her chin came up while she continued to massage cream into the skin below her cheekbones like someone trying to recall the ache and shape of a pulled tooth. But she went on too long; the black arm grew tired, I kittled up. My Duchess's eyes slid, the muscles at the corners of her mouth twitched; I was halfway to the bedroom door at 'grab' and by the jamb at 'him'. And though – 'go on, go on!' – the goddaughter pursued me, she did so fatalistically, from lumber to falter, along two sides of a courtyard while I waited, sniffing and twitching, a convenient stretch ahead. She did not appeal. She did not even look up. But in a kind of communion with the floor, squat-stumbled towards it, knees bending, arms out; she ended on all fours, head hanging. A trap? She looked as solid as a stone bench. I shrugged. I moved on.

Though just why did my Duchess wish to keep me in? Punishment? What had I done? And why had I seen spite in her eyes – or was I misled by her greasy lids and cheeks? And why, as unsought reward for my escape and cautious appearance, did our artist, hat all lit up, thrust Saint George at me and seem gratified by my reaction – a sneeze, some blinking and a retreat – though it was more the fear of hot candlewax and the shudder-shadows than the subject matter that caused it? Note, the forty-second engraving has been marked, possibly completed, but the light and my position made it hard to tell; the image was inscrutably maculate, reflected spots, had lines disappearing into shadow, could equally have been a cat's head or a giant moth or . . .

'Good boy!'

Summoning me to his writing table he fitted a roll of paper round my tail or rather, vice versa, he pushed my tail into the roll.

Naturally I do not know exactly what the message said. Naturally I knew who it was for. I dealt with an itch on my chin.

'Yayaya.'

Reluctantly I traipsed back through his bedroom, along the corridor, down the stairs, round the courtyard the long way – and stopped. The black girl sat, sleepily hugging her knees, outside my Duchess's door. She was, I think, shawl-tented in a sheet. Was she guarding the room? Had she been excluded? Did she need me to get in?

In the dark night I clambered up two columns and, on still warm rooftiles, took the tail-message over to the other side and swung down to the window (already seen in the business of the ant), slipped through the bars and briskly rapped before I had properly made out either my Duchess or that the pane and frame, though ajar, had been fixed.

She was sit-lying, ankles crossed, one hand squashing her cheek, the other, hanging down the side of the upholstered chair, holding, apparently just between thumb and index finger, a hand-mirror. This last swung slightly, like a displeasingly uncertain pendulum. I got her to stop it by rattling the tail-paper on the glass – but no more.

Chatteringly, I tackled crack and sneck on my own; a patient fiddle, an increasingly sore finger. When at last, with a soft shriek, I managed to squeeze in, she uncrossed her ankles but showed no interest in my insistently proffered *pupa* (hurt). I sniff-sneezed, vaulted lightly up on to her belly and examined my own hand there. I was aware that she sighed, that she rubbed between her eye and nose; then she lifted my tail and tugged off the letter – not as he had put it on, but unrolling the paper like a bandage. To read, she groaned and sat up. Having read, she stayed still. The contents? I repeat, I never read them but surmise is easy: 'Your Grace, I have made some poor efforts, forty-two of them, to correspond, at least in some measure, to your generous hospitality during my six weeks on your property, by engraving some whimsical images on the copper plates your Grace provided.' Or something of that sort. There may have been a brief interlude about her person. It may have been more rather than less fruity in style. It was not very long. Some five lines. And his signature large but in abbreviated form.

'Shoo,' said my Duchess.

I dropped to the floor.

With blobby care, she replied. I blew on my finger as she would blow on the ink. I scratched. The note, a short thing, took longer to dry than to write. She waved the sheet of paper, dabbed experimentally with a small finger, grunted. Mark, she merely held out the folded paper – I had to go and get it – and sent me back – 'No, no. You came in that way, you go back that way.' – via the window. But with my hand on the bars she decided to have doubts – '*Espe . . . creo . . .*' (Wait . . . I think . . .), here exhaling resignedly, crossing her arms over her breasts, then frowning and holding out her writing hand. A small, purplish-black ink stain on her finger. I shook my head. I was not going to have a session of crumpled draughts. Not *more* letters. So that in effect, already up on the roof, I agreed with her; this last letter was superfluous. Accordingly, after further reflection in his bedroom – a gift is a gift – I slipped the note between sheep's-skull jaws, made it snug in horsehair.

Our artist had finished, was now in a plethora of numbering and titling though, and this is a humble detail, he seemed more troubled by his spelling than anything else; the artist broke off, raised his closed eyes towards the ceiling, mouthed his alphabet, wrote. I saw him fix the final order of 7, 8, 9. Go to 36 next – for relief? I was then, though in briskly-worn candlelight, occasionally troubled by his stocky legs – once he stopped to beckon me with and then give me his index finger, pulling me forward – the first non-artist to see the set and final order of the engravings. I had before seen some singly, some suddenly, some taking shape, some runs or sections, but I had not seen the whole six weeks and now that I could, I suspended judgement; all eyes, no whys, I had little choice. Certain impressions – the rawness in some of the scratches, the terribly close texture of some of the scoring, the tilt of the series – caused an at odds sensation of mental shrinking; my brain like an aged apple, wrinkling as I watched.

Consider for a moment 13 or, if you prefer, 26. Here my Duchess dances. There I sit on a small cart in the dusk. How cold I look on my boat! I examined the hinge – for the lines and the flight path. Examined the shocking, puzzling 42. Then the first. Where else does he use the stone watertank? I marry them. I examine her tufted moons. I pose with the goddaughter. I trap a toad. I avoid a housekeeper. And the guacamayo! His use of mirrors, above a bather and a measured diner. And all my different hats. And her moths. I flee from rennet. She washes. I remained uncooked, my mother is roasted. She rolls a stocking. I fish dogs with a carefully-cut key.

I have never timed eggs. Too dry. Too particled. But I remained there, cocking my head, squinting, peering at her *zíngaros*, his senior lady, stepping back, crouching close to examine myself examining her, turned from supper to supper, a good, spluttering half-candle's worth before I started blinking. At what? At his dispatch? At the hairs of his eyebrows like cockroach legs? At his ending? At my own forty-nine-fold incidentalness? Nothing so marked. I felt a certain dull surprise, a certain dull alarm as if I were a furry sand-clock and almost run-through. I found I had quit the engraving room, crossed his letter and oils room but had petered out in his bedroom. In front of me was a bath of scummy water and a gross, charged sponge. I started. My sinews jerked. I turned. And robbed, tightly doll-cradling it in my right arm, the sheep's brain-case.

Consider the roof a footbridge between artist and Duchess; first up the slope, as steep as if you were to draw lines from the s of slope and the p of steep to the first o of the roof above, then along the ridge – the short leg of an L – to turn at right angles to take the long leg, then down the other or outer slope, from first tile to last a linear distance of some hundred and six feet. I must, though it was not my impression, have dawdled as I toted my sheep's-skull, chattering inconclusively and wondering, from the obtuse clonks it had given me as I clambered up, what to do with it. There were sidelines and outlines as well; the times I had come that way, the skull definitely not an offering to her – in any case the letter was still between those bony jaws – but there was nowhere obvious to store it.

At the very last of the roof ridge, wanting to potter down the reverse slope but still resentfully considering those whitish eyesockets, the hairs on my back sprung. Pins piercing, filaments burning, I spun, reared up and struck two-handed with the skull. I hit something – at least heard a sharp click – felt a gross buffet of air of a wing-tipped shadow, hissed as I crouched at the stench of carrion and, with my head shaking and my mind a jumble of talons and beak, I peered into the darkness.

The shock – nightmares are private, the gall of the preying fowl! – delayed my pulse for two, three, four beats. Instead my eyes parodied my heart – cave-wing, cave-wing – until muscle and blood came together in a squitter and a leap. My deductions, that I had feared an owl more than a night bustard, came *much* later. I never heard that skull fall – and in a moment, short enough to strangle a scream, using all my flattened limbs and tail, I fled.

Headfirst over coping and eaves, my impetus downwards leaked outwards; whirling my tail, torturing my back, I just – the final joint of the three middle fingers of my right hand – got hold of one of the window bars and swung-squirmed in. Only here I found that my Duchess had fixed the wretched window again, as exactly and rigidly as before. I squashed my face against the pane, ineffectually tried to scratch the glass with my bared teeth, did with my imploring fingers make the surface squeal but inside, made vaporous not by my eyes but by mosquito netting round her bed, my Duchess slept. There was no sign – and I craned and hopped and squinted – of her goddaughter. When I panic I sneeze. My Duchess stirred; in sleep she cupped her left bub with the expression, appalling, supercilious, of an enraptured violoncellist.

Now my pulse was hopelessly centred on my eardrums. At the base of the wall a cicada worked. In the distance unconcerned frogs croaked. Chattering, I turned and examined mortar and bars. The finger that I had previously used to open the window throbbed. I was not sure. But I did not think a nightmare bird of prey would be able to prise me out of my barred cubbyhole – too much flap and those claws, ideal for snail shells, would find horizontal movement crossed out by vertical wrought iron and me more mobile than a slime and jelly mollusc. With my back to the panes I rolled my head on my shoulder till my temple touched glass.

The gap between window and frame might have been sufficient for a supple snake – not a toad but the slenderest of bootlace snakes. Did I have revenge in mind? I held my breath. Bah. Under other circumstances I might have saved her. There was – I scrabbled round – a dark shadow or a crack on the barley-twist bedpost. Here, however, before I could get it to slither, I became aware of another sort of projection, neither reflection nor shadow; by shifting and twitching I got a monkeyish shape to squat at the base of the bed. Mine. Note my stolid white-face and receding hair reflected in the foreground in the thick pane. By pulling her sheet towards me I would have bared her body, soft tug by soft tug, letting the sheet slide down the steeper slopes of flesh on its own. My tail is not a cutting lash. I blinked. As a comfortable nest her sheet would have done well. My lids were almost closed, my mind's eye, from shock and fatigue, likewise. The sound of insects and reptiles provided some comfort; carefully securing my tail, I settle-huddled on the stone ledge.

I used sometimes – circuitously but with short cuts – to wonder what would be for me; would I pass through alum solution to share the guacamayo's perch? be put in a glass cabinet? get a dry branch and be always climbing towards a corner? Or would I have a small, round-headed tombstone? Here lies a sapajou? Be placed next to the lapdog? Or neither of these, not stuffed, not buried, but given a shovel-scrape, carrion-shallow grave in the scrub? Or just tail swung and hefted into the sea? I think I prefer this last, hup and splash, but it does not matter at all and I now find these idle thoughts pests, irritating for what they are, like ticks or fleas. Be less marmoreal, white-face.

What I hate now is that twitter, that shiver and spasm of blood, brain and muscles when I wake from stunned sleep; grate, hearth, it is like the raking out of some cupidic undertaker's dream. A noisy hunting swallow dipped. I blinked. Late, I secured my tail. I sniffed. My Duchess slept on, though sulking at first insect light. I picked gum from my left eye but broke off, prodded by a swollen bladder, to peer – cautiously – from the bars and then shin scramble up to the roof.

I was squeamishly treating my hands – they crack in this climate – when, almost at the same time, I made out the bleached sheep's-skull to my left and heard to my right, as faint as suspicion, sounds of the artist's going. I ceased the spray and drip. I woke more. Two-legged, thus at a hirple, I swayed as far along the roofridges as I dared, ineffectively shadowing his cloak, his hat – was that the gleam of seaweed-black coach door? – uncomfortably aware of restless horses, of hoofs on grit, of trickle and creak and gate; but all I actually saw – was that a forward shadow, a silhouette in the short avenue of poplars? – after a relatively chilly spell on that rooftop promontory was a trundle or a wisp of dust in the ground mist, far beyond the puffs of green, which may have been caused by his departing carriage, already nearer the dawn and the ferry than the *palacete*.

Rid of his fleshy presence, my skin prickled, mildly. I scratched and waited for the sun, from halo-rim through grim blush to half-disc, first blue and then glare. A gull soared. Roof-dew sparkled. The crane and other foreshortened figures moved below, hastily seen since I needed some arm-waving care against slipping on my way back. Remarkable how dry the sheep's-skull

154

was. After some dull deliberation on dew, terracotta and bone while relieving my bowels I picked it up and stole back along the way I had come the night before, from owl swoop to the tiles over the artist's abandoned bedroom – though here I did not go inwards to the courtyard but outwards, I'd say over the bath, to look out over Doñana. There I sat and separated paper from jaw, horsehair from cranium.

That skull I doubted over, sconce askant – a sheepish life, a possible weapon – but quickly decided that only a feckless go-between would need an ovine jaw-bone against nocturnal birds of prey. Accordingly, having flexed my toes against the maxilla, I slid my foot under the chin and flicked; the skull tumbled, rolled, chipped a tile, chipped itself, then rollick-leapt down and off the roof. A second or two later there was a light-boned dry-grass sound followed by a satisfying calcic click.

The horsehair I tossed aside for future nesting birds or adventurous rodents. Her last undelivered note to him I conned but, despite the time I took to do that – and I am a slow reader, have to take my finger, follow the cursive links your grace, your correspondence – and to cram it beneath a rooftile, then to clamber down for a brief surprise – no one had come to the artist's rooms – and then to approach my Duchess's suite with some care, as slowly as a servant with a laden tray, I found her still not dressed. Amazing woman; she drank hot chocolate and wolfed chopped, unpeeled apple draped in folds of thick, clay-white honey.

She had just enough time to dress (but not to make-up) before vomiting. Nerves? Pride? The attraction of a purgative? What startled me – booming whoops, slaughterhouse lowing below and throat-sectioning hacks above the splatter – brought an anxious ankling of housekeeper and maids.

But wait. Having rinsed out her mouth, having wiped her forehead with a proffered lavender-soaked handkerchief – while others scurried to open my window, to wring out wet cloths – my Duchess, squid-white, squid-elastic about the lips, tugged a strand of vomited-on hair from her cheek and turned for the door.

Note how decided her walk becomes. In consequence, she sheds confusion and people, uncertain servants in her room and the cloisters, the dismayed housekeeper – *mi niña, mi niña* – as late as the unmade cardinal's campaign bed and finally her goddaughter, straggle-faltering in the fust of turpentine and drying oils. Any other possible witness to her reactions to the artist's correspondence was excluded by catching the unsheddable capuchin firmly between door-jamb and her lower leg. Revise that unsheddable; naturally, delicate as a reversing clock mechanism, I retreated as soon as pressed.

But she did not let me slip backwards. She bent, grabbed the scruff of my neck as an infant assures a fat-handled spoon and tossed me at her goddaughter.

Surely I had begun somewhere about there – airborne – though here unrescued, unravelling. I caught at an ineffectual black arm, a warding off rather than a flesh branch, and quickly swung, onefold unfold, round the goddaughter's neck, my chin on her bushy hair. Was I really afraid she would see the engraving room door close? But why? With a shriek of protest, shrill as any hinge, I tried to cover her eyes with my hands before the inner bar slid to. With a dank thud, it did.

That cannot have been instantaneous despair. I had become a *mono-moño*, a sapajou-chignon.

'*Estate quieto*,' said the peevish girl, plucking at one of my hands and indeed, despite the brevity of the paralysis, it had degenerated into something brisk and lewd, if limp.

Did I wait for the sounds of my owner's reactions – laughter, murmur, kicked copper plates? Or imagine her – did she lift or crouch and peer? – examining his engravings one by one? Did my Duchess whirl?

No, no. I became aware of a dull, repetitive rasping; candle flint. I could not bear the wait. As soon as I imagined a burst of light, a yellowish lime leaf behind my eyes, I turned at once, dropped to the floor via the goddaughter's firm, salient buttocks and fled – veering away from the housekeeper, the old lady morosely strangling a suet-coloured sponge – for fresher air.

I wish I could say that the sapajou then thought the matter out, calibrated copper, candlelight and reactions, even adopted the attitude of a thinker – but I did not. Delicate-footed but dull I traipsed downwards, circumnavigated my familiar courtyard to sit a while on the sleeping tortoise and from my hillock-seat observe the cat making a coy game of something soft and rollable – a dead rat or a gift of rabbit skin – and the peacock and peahen pondering the prospect of seed in the grit while the goat, belly like a pipebag, remained silent and aloof but at the full extent of its tether, a good yard short of the stone tank where it liked to rest its chin.

The tortoise shell needed oil again, its stars resembled huge, dry limpets. I picked, felt cracks, stroked a rough, livid patch of carapace with the fourth finger of my right hand – but I had already stopped when the old reptile woke. Its eyes, like rained-on black currants, fixed on something; it heaved itself up, shell grating, on to its stubby legs. What had passed through its mind?

It lumbered a yard or two, the movement, as if it lacked a joint, a stick not on a hoop but on a straight-edged box, obliging me to snatch and cling, but only for four dragging steps; the tortoise halted, unable to sustain memory or impulse. Or perhaps its myopia had made a pebble turn into a tidbit. That wrinkled neck, wrinkled as a bellows bag, drooped, those eyes closed; my seat was no longer in shade.

Accordingly, squinting irritably, I exchanged shell for stone, flitted back across the courtyard to the balustrade on the first floor, picked a grape from the vine, smeared the bloom, skinned it, found it not too sweet. Women passed. Ants harvested something. Without remark a maid swept up a leaf I crushed and dropped for her. A bandy-legged manservant, trying to untangle a curious, square harness, did not notice me. Nor did those carrying the artist's (emptied) bath. Nor his folded bed-drapes. For surely I was a more or less amusing articulated fur ornament, not an affront? I am a monkey; with neat, precise hands, an old man's head and large, touching eyes.

And yet my Duchess sought me out. Her gaze, as she strode down the cloister, she kept fixed on the far end where – I checked – there was no one at all; but she pulled up exactly by me to present herself in thrusting profile and begin working on her lips, now like a fish, now sucking her tongue. I cocked my right eye. The left twitched. Both widened, the left still hapless. My skin also tightened at her delicacy in achieving the tension required to have a bubbled sheet of saliva hang inside her lips. She squeezed the saliva into a large, larger bubble; then took tooth-snapping, cheek-flecked pleasure in bursting the transparent swell. Her tongue licked, her mouth puckered, assumed a twist as she turned full-face, her right eye mocking, the other a glazed deal knot. I started. She, with a marmishly-timed index finger, rapped hard on my nose, a sharp chopworth of sound.

'Sit!'

I sneezed, she nodded.

'*No te escondiste, ¿verdad?*'

Esconder? Hide was that? Her tone, hoarse, matter-of-fact, inquisitive, was too hard for me. Why hadn't I *hidden*?

'*Pues escóndete ya.*'

Oh, I did not understand this. An imperative, a now. But hide? Where?

And what had I done? Her skirts slithered on, my shadow shrank a little more. My image had been borrowed for a series of engravings. That did not make me responsible. Did not make *me* an intruder.

I did not know then that a bandy-legged servant was already struggling to wrap the plates in greased paper and chamois and put them in a trunk of leather and wood and wicker in which they were to go north, locked and strapped, some days later when my Duchess also left, on persistent rumours of an outbreak of fever.

I was not taken. Which matters most in the sense that I am still here; was not, say, perched on a green and bleached leather trunk when the flames began.

I certainly *tried* to go with her, certainly tasted blood, but was twice removed from her carriage, once by an ungloved servant, then by a gloved one, then chased off with zeal by a small boy wielding a sharp-pronged, over-heavy rake. Rather than be chased again, I retired to the roof and while the huge circus of my Duchess's departure upped, I practised; more silhouette than sapajou, I followed shadows about the roof, always shadow side, often with my toes in the sun but varying from the easy (advance with the shadow) to the difficult (retreat inside it). I also hung from the eaves like an old fruitbat, my skin feeling as fuzz-mossy, as crumbling dry, as the stuff on the north-facing roof.

Well protected by pelitre and other plants, some burnt and swung like incense, somewhere in the middle of folded sheets and spread dustsheets, fast carriages and top-heavy carts, bulwarked by hatboxes, toiletboxes and trunks, my Duchess disappeared. Shutters squealed. Furniture was dragged. Dogs whined. The permanent servants began their campsite in the kitchen court-yard. *Did* I see her again? Was I looking? The black goddaughter certainly – giving imperious instructions on some *nécessaire*. But she? I am not sure I really did. Come, a little more than push and less than kin. There was a personage, glimpsed, a distant, ghastly mummified figure, with a hat tied for a wind – though there was none, only swung smoke. She entered a carriage with more difficulty than ceremony – those bandages were tightly bound – and rattled off. My food dish is put down, full of tarnished fruit. The cat inspects chicken viscera and fish heads. The peahen's scurry becomes a doleful peck. The goat has worms. The tortoise begins to turn its head.

At last – relief from all that prophylactic huff and off – here comes the forty-second! His correspondence, doubtless – but decidedly their grace. The skin of my cheeks crawling, my spine con-tracting, my lower teeth clamping on my upper lip. And surely these things were not entirely due to his suggestion and my impatience? They *were* late that year. Though let me be clear – you cannot be prescient about an annual occurrence, only experienced, only informed. The hairs on my arms rose, not through fear, these had a softer, more languorous, pleasured quirk; delighted, peering hard, grinning like a jaunty turnip, I limited myself to performing my triple movement of traditional welcome: ankle, knee and thigh. Sun-sparked wings: the quick-stitching flight of a hundred thousand dragonflies rising from flat wetlands. Glinting needles pulling rapid gold threads in dun-dust and blue-shot silk, an undulation in the phantasmagoric whole between a slow-moving banner and a shudder. Hypnotic yes, but less gold gossamer – let's to his scratch.

42

THE DUCHESS'S

DRAGONFLY

———

LIBELULA DE LA DUQUESA

OR

ODONATA

THE VERY LAST ENGRAVING, READER, IN PART
named after the order to which the dragonfly belongs,
includes a familiar sapajou squatting at the base of a
palm tree in a masturbatory or at least loinishly
secretive way. Though it can't, not at that length, I
think, be the glans; is that one more walnut I have
between thumb and forefinger? Have I just shaken
it? I am not sure.

Around but mostly above the capuchin are some
five hundred dragonflies, shown from a plethora of
angles; there is – and I have, mentally, turned the
etching upside down, laid it on both sides – a most
decided vortex, a cornucopia to the whirl of
dragonflies with the tail or horn tip not far from the

possible walnut.

Surely he does not suggest they have come *from* that pair of brain- and boat-shaped shells? That would be fantastical. A dragonfly comes from a ferocious nymph; it is a housefly that comes from a maggot.

Stop. The palm, to the right, provides a vertical. It is all trunk, the fronds have been lopped. The viewer, that is, is on a level with a monkey sitting on and looking down from the edge of the roof while wearing a gloomy giant's wide-brimmed hat. Accordingly, the sapajou in the engraving looks even more hunched, its white face unclear; but its posture is pathetic enough, the contents of whatever it is between its fingers sufficiently worrying for it to be ignorant of the rising sycamore spin turning up and to the left.

Listening?

I don't know. Susceptible, suspicious, I have even examined the spaces *between* the veined insect wings, carefully sought membrane and braking feathers, a jeering artist. But I think there is no back-handed intent of that sort. In part because, look, one dragonfly shows its belly as if separated from the viewer by a pane of glass.

I'd have taken a stone. But there, I mean on the roof, when the dragonflies emerged from the *marismas* in early September, I was more sanguine, considered the whole series as well as the last engraving, though a little distracted by the tinted, scintillant clouds approaching the *palacete*.

These clouds began to break up; particles in a

greyish swim. A certain blackness – angle, shadow, sun – and an inner violence as my dragonflies shot forward, hovered, darted, drifted upwards, swept sideways and down on flattish arcs.

They do blunder. They are, despite their rapidity, easily snatched by swifts and even seagulls. They are inquisitive enough to bite, that is their eyesight is acute but also acutely limited. They bite to find out but do not seem to see that other dragonflies have bitten. I do not mind – the bite is brisk rather than painful – and I enjoy watching them settle on my fur. On the rooftiles dragonflies rested; others streamed over the ridge. And it was here I properly came back to his Odonata; I wished to see how the invaded courtyard looked. I could recall masses of dragonflies but no swarm shape to them, no narrow source on the ground, no order; they have not even the loose looping of locusts or the sticky interest of houseflies.

As I scurried up the roof, I glimpsed, to my left, a slim, sand-brown dash. A dragonfly on its tile hunting-pad had not seen the lizard. There was a quick, moist snap. The lizard raised its head but not to look out for me; its jaws had stuck on the dragonfly, its efforts to swallow what it had caught crosswise of the most clumsy. I pounced, feinting to my left. Instantly the lizard dropped its tail – it is a long time since I was misled by that – and I let it waddle-squirm uphill to my right hand and grasped it firmly round the midriff. With deliberation I picked up the excited tail and pushed it against the stump, at the same time squeezing that slack bag of viscera. The reptile wheezed but the dragonfly, the blue body mangled, its wings crushed, was stuck at the jaw hinges.

I desisted. The lizard continued to play dead. Other *libelulas* hovered and darted about me. I stayed still. A weather-vane monkey in black cast-iron? No. As I considered the insect, the lizard and its still vigorously worming tail, I understood that it was more than pointless for me to look for any swarm of dragonflies; they and I ignore any such whirlwind shape. Though let me be fair to myself; I had wondered if he had been more observant than me. A dragonfly paused on me, nipped and moved on. Very well. The fat reptile and the destroyed insect I tossed off the roof in the direction of the skull. The tail I let drop to watch it writhe and go still. A lymphish drop at the raw extremity attracted no curiosity except mine, briefly. What, at the end of that slender limpness, did the under-pink and cyclops aspect remind me of?

I did not wait to find out but crossed the roof to sit on the inner slope like a dull servant on the dunes. Had he then – hear the huzz and waves of wings – made of his correspondence a vindictive story? Had he furrowed her? Shelled me? Loathed himself? She soars, he is me? These things are entirely possible, but swarm-like. Look again – through her headdresses and poses and more *menudo* body than real – at that last engraving. The dragonfly (pepper-red I think) that shows its underside to the viewer is considerably larger than the squatting monkey. Perspective? Certainly. Seasonal?

Of course. But was that *her* dragonfly? And how? In what sense? *She* was not a dragonfly. She did not *own* the dragonfly. And I could hardly think an episode had wings, engravings nervures. Or could I? Could I? I was interrupted by the stretched thump of the peacock's tail, quills protesting, feathers trembling. Combative? Jealous? It could not sustain the effort. Sheafed, it pecked.

Below me the cat boxed. I saw goat and dragonfly, tortoise and dragonfly. Dragonflies nosed about shell and columns, horns and arches. Dragonflies rested on grapes. Dragonflies investigated palms. Dragonflies bumped on windows. Their stiffness and their colouring, plush and glazed web, lends them something mechanical. Each pair of wings can beat independently of the other. They can fly backwards, hover, turn where they are. But see them over water! The mottled gold and white fish tended down, thought sluggishly of danger rather than food while above them the exhilarating reflection and flash of dragonflies made for a multiple twin skimming. Blue, green, red – and pale, sun-caught gold everywhere, a teeming, a whirring . . . there *is* no collective noun. A flock? A cloud? No, the effect on water, as quick as westerly sunbeams flickering on an east-twisted sea – sparks angled, sparks reflected – is not of clouds. Nor do the insects resemble coloured paper rising from fire. Nor does the crackle of fire sound the same way. The crepitation in my ears, akin to sherbet poppling on my drums, was caused by airy arithmetic; thirty beats a second, two pairs of wings, a low estimate of two thousand dragonfly in the courtyard, makes for one hundred and twenty thousand beats each cloistered second.

Too much excitement, too much movement; my heart. For contrast and a slower pulse I picked on a dragonfly that had settled at the right-hand corner of the stone tank and, though distracted by the extraordinary twisted grass-stalk manner of a mating pair to the left, concentrated on it alone. But what did I expect? It rested there for some seconds, tail cocking, before I realised that the image retained by my eye had become a flecked, empty circle, that the dragonfly's absence was left like the pale inset of a ghost; then further back another dragonfly appeared, less outlined, more opaque; then further back still, another, smaller, darker – and suddenly multiple, like winged carbon specks.

Ah. For a moment there I thought that, as well as being open to understanding, I had understood. Absurd. More sensation (brain yeast and headskin) than perception (clear eyes and sentences). I had thought, just for a moment, that there was, somewhere between appetite and pride, puzzlement and desire, even more difficult to gather and hold in mind than forty-two engravings, a tense, slippery mental clutching that reaches a state in which desire curves through a sense of loss and issues as a zestful pang of longing.

An illusion. From a dour artist's point of view a drop of water is in the first place a colourless eye. That pepper-red dragonfly is about to soar past his black, candled brim. Is that what I find alarming? Much more than his or hers. Its going?

Well, I am a cowardly capuchin, would rather watch admirable wingspans thrum than throw off a shudder myself. I have preferred to make out the bodies under the translucent wings that bear them up and push them on and to do so with more time and less passion, more justice and less press, than by scoring the clash of intimacies on metal. I am, compared to him, *caballito del diablo*? Hardly.

I am capuchin, witness and image. Only image. And, of course, now with my mind backed by sun, palatial sparks, pretty flies and the gleam of incised copper, I realise that what I said at the beginning is false. I said I had been roused into the verbal aping of engraved lines by my fear of forgetting them. But it was my fear of being left alone with such arrogant, exacting memories that did it. *That* was my only swarm.

Here they are then, I hand them on. I believe that successive pulls blunt the images on the copper plates, repeated pressing softens them. That is not displeasing, though I prefer to free them and free myself. I can now turn my eyes on other things, look out from here for the last time with an ingratiating, ironically Socratic air.

There is no creature as sudden in its taking-off as my Duchess's dragonfly.